THE POLISH GHOST

by

Nicholas M. Krohn

Dedicated to my mom,
who has shown me how to persevere, who has loved
me unconditionally, and who has always been there
for me, no matter how hard the road was. I hope I am
at least half as good a parent to my children as you
were to me.

Table of Contents

PROLOGUE:

Shot

Aleksander Kurtz never expected being shot would be so excruciatingly painful. He had known several men who had experienced it before, including his own father. None of them, however, described the anguish quite as keenly as he felt it in those terrible moments.

There are many stories where an individual didn't live past one bullet piercing his fragile frame. Aleksander would be among the privileged few to tell his tale even after being shot *twice*.

Still, in unspeakable pain, he did his best to breathe deeply and to keep himself calm. Panicking would not only not help him but would make the situation more dire. He needed a level head and a steady heart for what he was about to do.

He recalled the instructions his father had given him just in case something like this was to happen. First, he needed to clean the wound in his leg. He was not to try and dig the bullet out. The bullet was only to be removed if it would cause more damage than leaving it there. Aleksander again examined his leg, and from what he could tell, no major arteries had been struck. He was an amateur at this, however, and knew it would be better to find professional medical attention as soon as he possibly could.

But for now, he was to rely on himself. Once he

cleaned it, he would need to patch up his leg to ensure the blood flow was stopped. Blood loss and infection were the two most likely things he would die from. He would do everything he could to avoid either fate.

The tourniquet, he remembered, was a simple yet life-saving device in this kind of circumstance. His father had seen plenty of these in his day, and Aleksander knew well of it due to his father's teachings.

Aleksander slipped off his belt, thankful that his pants were tight enough without it. He looped the belt around his leg, right above the gunshot wound. He then steeled himself for the pain he was about to go through.

In one fluid motion, he quickly tightened the belt around his leg. A miserable gasp escaped his throat as he felt the surge of agony explode through his leg.

But he couldn't stop now. In order for it to work, he needed his belt to be so tight that it would cut off blood flow. If he kept bleeding out, he would die.

Pain was better than death.

Tightening the belt wasn't even the worst part. After all, circulation still hadn't been cut off. Now came the most egregious part of the tourniquet. He was to take something thin and strong, place it under his belt, and twist it until circulation was truly halted. He found a short but stout stick that would do the trick. Every turn would be horrible, but he had to do it.

Once Aleksander finished and was able to stifle

his cries, he began praying. He knew he could not continue without the Lord with him in this. He prayed that he could still walk and, if need be, run. He prayed the wound wouldn't get infected. He prayed the tourniquet had been applied correctly and that he wouldn't bleed to death. He prayed he would make it the rest of his journey.

Aleksander tried to stand and immediately cried out before collapsing back on the ground. His leg was worse off than he thought. Just by putting pressure on his leg, he quickly felt tremendous pain branch through the bone in it.

"The bullet is lodged in my femur." He realized grimly. This made things much more difficult. He wouldn't be able to walk with just a tourniquet. He would need a splint.

Again, he took deep breaths and tried to calm himself down. He knew how to make splints. It would be hard, but doable.

He couldn't quit now. He **wouldn't** quit now.

Even if he was going to die, Aleksander knew he wouldn't quit until his final breath. Even if a dozen bullets riddled his body, he was ready to continue his mission and see it to the very end.

His mission was Liliana.

The most beautiful girl in Poland.

He was to save her from Nazi-occupied Zaginiony.

CHAPTER ONE:

Liliana

Liliana Hodor. Aleksander thought she was exceptional. She was a young woman who had the most magnetic personality. She was incredibly likable, did well in school, was very kind, thoughtful, and respectful, and held most other qualities that people found favorable. Liliana was the kind of fourteen-year-old that people just wanted to be around. Especially when she smiled. For she was also amazingly beautiful. Everyone praised her as such.

Liliana seemed perfect.

But if you look hard enough and long enough, flaws always surface.

Her choice in boyfriends was terrible. Like many of the boys she dated, she only looked skin deep. The ideal boyfriend, in her mind, had to be just as attractive as she was. She only clung to the arms of the most handsome boys, and always for the worse. Though they had charming looks, many of those boys had glaring blemishes. Several of her boyfriends had no character or dignity. Others had no respect for her parents. And all of them were lazy sluggards who didn't know what the word "work" even meant.

Thankfully, Liliana's parents were wise and strict, forbidding Liliana to proceed too far in a relationship without their blessing. None of her past boyfriends ever met their approval.

Aleksander intended to change that.

"Stop ogling my girl, Kurtz." Piotr shoved Aleksander as he walked by his seat. He had caught Aleksander staring at Liliana.

In response, Aleksander simply scoffed. Liliana was as much Piotr's girl as she was Aleksander's. Piotr had lasted merely a week before Liliana's parents told their daughter that Piotr was not going to continue to be her boyfriend.

Handsome and tall? Yes. Honorable and diligent? Absolutely not.

Piotr had heard Aleksander scoff and gave the short boy a glare as he sat down in his seat next to Aleksander.

"What?" He snorted in a pig-like manner. "You think you have a chance with her? A dwarf mute who looks like he was raised by ogres?"

Aleksander's eye twitched as he slowly turned his head towards Piotr.

"If you use the term 'ogres' for my parents one more time, I'll throw you out the window," he warned in a quiet, dark tone.

"Ha!" Piotr laughed. "Like you even could! You're a midget, Kurtz! Just try it!"

Aleksander turned away from Piotr again, ignoring his challenge.

Apparently, that angered the poor fool. He leaned over to Aleksander. "Your parents are worse than ogres, Kurtz. They—"

That was it. Piotr had crossed the line.

Aleksander stood up from his desk and snatched Piotr by the collar of his uniform. Aleksander then yanked Piotr from his seat to the floor and began walking to the window, dragging Piotr across the floor.

The entire rest of the class immediately went silent and turned their attention to the two boys. Piotr actively tried to pull himself free, but Aleksander's grip was iron. Piotr then punched Aleksander in the gut, but the small boy didn't even flinch. And Piotr realized grimly that his hand suddenly felt like he had punched a solid oak tree.

"No, no, no, Kurtz!" Piotr pleaded right as they reached the window. "I'm sorry!"

"Too late," Aleksander told him calmly.

In one fluid motion, Aleksander tossed him out of the window.

Aleksander was short, yes, but Aleksander was strong.

And he did not tolerate the mockery of his parents.

The whole classroom gawked as they witnessed Piotr fly out the window and crash into the bushes. Piotr let out a mournful wail as if he were dying.

The school was only a one-story building. He had fallen about three feet.

Aleksander shook his head at Piotr's continued cries before returning to his desk. Just then, the teacher, Mr. Laris, walked into the room.

"To your seats!" He announced. "I apologize for

being late." The children quickly obeyed, though many kept glancing at the window.

Mr. Laris then noticed the empty desk next to Aleksander. "Where's Piotr?" He asked.

Then, on cue, Piotr made another groan from outside. Mr. Laris looked out the window with a heavy sigh.

"Piotr, I haven't the slightest idea what you're doing in those bushes, but that's quite enough. Get to your seat. Play hide-and-seek on your own time after school."

No one, including Piotr, said a word about what had happened. For Piotr, Aleksander judged that he knew the reason. After all, how much reputation would Piotr lose if he admitted that the shortest boy in school tossed him out a window like he was a ragdoll?

For lunch, the children were allowed half an hour of freedom to enjoy their lunches and rest from the curriculum. Most all the kids ate outside to experience the fresh, spring air as they ate. Of course, everyone ate in their cliques, their group of friends. This included Liliana. She sat on the grassy knoll not too far from the school building and ate with various other girls.

Suddenly, a shadowy chill fell over them. They all turned to see Aleksander, who had appeared out of nowhere without a sound.

"Excuse me," he interjected formally.

All of the girls stared at him with wide, worried eyes. Especially Liliana. Aleksander had never spoken to any of them before. For all they knew up until this point, he **couldn't** speak. Not to mention that Aleksander had thrown a boy nearly a foot taller than him out of a window earlier that morning. Seemingly unprovoked, as well.

The girls waited tensely for Aleksander to reveal why he was there. Their imagination took flight as to what he wanted. A quiet, small boy suddenly approaching them? Something he had never done before. After a violent outburst? Perhaps he had snapped. Perhaps the name-calling from the other boys had finally gotten to him. A few of the girls in Liliana's group who had gone along with the taunting were beginning to fret. Was he here for revenge?

Aleksander cleared his throat. "Miss Hodor, would you do me the honor of sitting with me while we eat our lunches?"

Liliana's eyebrows rose in surprise as she resisted the urge to let her mouth drop open. All of the other girls focused on her, curious as to how she would reject Aleksander.

But to everyone's shock, including Aleksander, she didn't reject his invitation.

"Sure," she said cooly, though she was still quite surprised. She stood up and walked towards Aleksander. Without another word, the two walked off together as gossip immediately started sprouting between the other girls.

Liliana was not sure why she had agreed to sit with Aleksander. It was a knee-jerk reaction. Had she had a bit more time to consider it, she mused that she probably would have said no. As she walked beside him, she felt like she was towering over him. The very top of his head only met her chin, and Liliana was not a particularly tall girl. No, Aleksander really was just small. He was very plain, as well. Nothing in his appearance was outstanding. He was the most average-looking person she had ever seen. Lastly, the boy never spoke. Liliana might have been able to forgive some of his appearance if he had a winning personality. If he was funny, if he was clever, if he was sensitive, if he was sweet, just *something*. But he was as quiet as a stone and, to her, had about as much personality. With all that information, she noted inwardly that she should not have agreed to have lunch with him.

But she did.

Because something gnawed at her when it came to Aleksander: he made Liliana curious.

Aleksander was shrouded in mystery. Part of that was from the fact that he rarely spoke, but there was more to it. Every day, after school, he quickly disappeared. There had been times when one or two of the other boys in the class had invited him to something, but Aleksander would always decline, saying he had work to do at home. He was the only boy in her class who hadn't flirted with her. In fact, if she recalled correctly, today was the first day he actually spoke directly to her.

And what about this morning?

This morning, she watched as a five-foot-one-inch

14

Aleksander threw a five-foot-eleven-inch Piotr out of the window with ***one arm!***

She glanced at Aleksander's arms. The school uniform was terribly modest. So much so that it often hid everyone's physique. If Aleksander did have muscular arms, the uniform kept that secret well.

But how else did he toss Piotr like that? Piotr was thin, but not ***that*** thin. She pondered that maybe Aleksander had used some trick of momentum to help him get Piotr off the ground and out the window.

But Liliana was cut off from her thoughts as she found they had reached their destination: the picnic table.

The picnic table was always vacant. For good reason, too. It was old, rickety, and smelled awful due to having been covered in numerous different foods and drinks over the years.

Liliana was about to rescind her agreement to eat with Aleksander and go back to her friends. Why would he even think this would be okay? As she was about to tell him to forget it, however, she noticed something different about the picnic table.

It was clean. It didn't smell. And, as Aleksander sat down on the bench, she realized that it wasn't creaking or looking like it was about to fall over. Someone had tightened it, strengthened it.

Then, to put a nice bow on it all, Aleksander manifested a large handkerchief. He spread it over where Liliana was designated to sit.

"No one's ever done that for me before." Liliana

15

was impressed, wondering if Aleksander himself was the one who brushed up the picnic table. She mentally renounced her decision to leave him and sat down on the handkerchief. She glanced to her left to see Aleksander praying over his meal. Feeling slightly guilty that she had not, she said a quick prayer over her meal.

The two took out their lunches and began eating.

No one said anything for a great deal of time.

Sitting side by side, neither of them looked at each other either.

Liliana found the awkward silence unbearable but had no idea what to say. She didn't know Aleksander at all. What could she talk about? The weather? Their respective lunches?

"So, you threw Piotr," Liliana blurted out.

Aleksander stopped eating and peered over at her. "I hope I didn't frighten you."

"Oh, no," Liliana sighed, relieved that they were getting into a conversation. "I mean, it was shocking. I don't know how you did that, but also…why did you do it?"

Aleksander turned back to his food. "He insulted my parents. I don't stand for that."

Liliana felt she was starting to tread on sensitive territory. "I'm very sorry. Piotr is rather crass. I didn't care for that side of him."

"Did he ever insult yours?" Aleksander questioned.

Liliana frowned guiltily. "Yes. More than a few times. I'm ashamed to say I didn't have the same

16

response as you."

"Throwing people out windows is usually discouraged anyway," Aleksander retorted, a hint of a grin on his face. Liliana gave a small laugh. She didn't necessarily find what Aleksander said funny. It was the fact that he had just tried to make a joke. It was a very unexpected thing for Liliana. She hadn't thought Aleksander could joke. It was a pleasant surprise for her to see that he wasn't completely made of stone.

At Liliana's laugh, Aleksander's smile grew. He knew he didn't smile much, so the expression felt foreign on his face. But it also felt very good to smile like that.

"I'm glad I asked her today." He congratulated himself. Aleksander had meant to ask her several weeks ago and tried, several times, to muster up the courage to speak to her. This time, he had triumphed over his fears and his inhibitions, and it was turning out very wonderful so far.

"How come I never hear you say anything?" Liliana suddenly inquired. "I don't mean to pry. I'm just rather curious."

"I don't have much to say, I suppose." Aleksander shrugged.

Liliana was unsatisfied with that answer. "Are you hiding something?"

"No."

"Some deep hurt, perhaps?" Liliana proposed.

"Everyone has hurt," Aleksander replied. "And I'm not hiding mine."

"Oh?" Liliana gave a mischievous grin. "Then share it with me."

"Okay. My mother died."

Liliana almost choked on her drink. "Oh! I didn't think you would actually—I'm so very sorry."

"Thank you." Aleksander nodded to her. "But it doesn't hurt as much as you think. She died when I was just a baby. I have no memory of her."

"Still, to grow up without a mother…" Liliana murmured sadly, wondering what life would be like without her own mother.

"I have a wonderful father." Aleksander's smile returned some. "And a heavenly Father, as well."

"You're very religious, aren't you?" Liliana observed.

"That's one way of saying it." Aleksander shrugged. "I do my best to honor Him."

"Lunchtime is over!" Mr. Laris called from one of the windows. "Everyone back inside!"

Liliana and Aleksander simultaneously did their best to finish their lunches quickly as everyone started heading inside.

"It was nice to finally get acquainted with you, Aleksander," Liliana told him as they began heading inside.

"It was very nice to sit and speak with you also, Miss Hodor," Aleksander responded.

"Formalities aside, please." Liliana smiled. "Call me Liliana."

"As you wish."

"Maybe we could talk again," Liliana suggested,

18

still very curious about him.

"Maybe, but I have to go very soon after school," Aleksander informed her.

"Why?"

"I need to tend to the horses," Aleksander explained.

"Horses?!" Liliana nearly screamed.

Aleksander raised his eyebrows in surprise.

Liliana grasped him by the shoulders. "You have horses? You *really* have horses?"

"Yes," Aleksander answered, marveling at her outburst.

"I've always wanted to see horses up close!" Liliana proclaimed. "Ever since I was a little girl!"

"Would you like to come by?" Aleksander offered.

"Oh, yes, please!" Liliana squealed. "Is that okay?"

"Yes, as long as you bring someone with you," Aleksander told her. "And you must know that I will have to work, so it won't be all fun and games."

"Bring someone with me?" Liliana blinked. "Why?"

"To act as a chaperone of sorts," Aleksander told her.

Liliana was taken aback. "Chaperone? Aleksander, we're not dating. We really just met today."

"I know," Aleksander replied without being phased at all. "But to be alone with the most beautiful girl in Poland? Rumors would spread

19

regardless of whether we were dating or not."

With that, Aleksander walked into the school.

"The most beautiful girl in Poland?" Liliana repeated in her head. *"This boy sure lays it on thick...but...I'd be lying to say that wasn't charming."*

CHAPTER TWO:

The Horse Ride

"Why do I have to come?" Albin Hodor asked his older sister. "You have hundreds of friends who could accompany you with your new boyfriend."

Liliana scoffed in response. "He's not even a *candidate* for my boyfriend."

"Then why are we walking to his house?"

"He has horses!" Liliana exclaimed happily.

"Who cares?"

"I care!" Albin snapped. Then, he asked again. "Which reminds me, why am I here and not the pack of girls that follow you around everywhere?"

"Everyone else is busy because they have lives. Unlike you." Liliana smirked at her eleven-year-old brother.

Liliana arrived with some expectations. Poland was familiar with horses, and there were stacks of books on the subject of horses. She knew a thing or two about them, but she had never experienced being up close to one. She dared to dream that Aleksander would let her ride one, though she knew that she might have to be firm and domineering with the animal. She didn't like the thought of being oppressive with such a beloved animal, but it was how things were done. Show any hesitancy or weakness, and it would be exploited. That was what she had read.

Coming over a hill, Liliana and Albin set their eyes on the Kurtz farm. It wasn't very impressive. Many of the farm buildings were clearly old. However, none of them seemed to be rickety or falling apart. They were in good shape due to being taken care of.

"Mr. Kurtz must be quite a jack of all trades." Liliana reasoned.

"He's a scary, strict, old war veteran." Albin gave her a quizzical glance. "And he's poor. If he were a jack of all trades, I don't think he'd live like this."

"Good grief, Albin, hold your tongue." Liliana reprimanded her brother. "I was complimenting his handiwork around here. Besides, even if he is poor and scary, be respectful. He fought for this country."

Liliana then nodded to herself, believing she had accomplished some well-needed instruction towards her brother. But as she began down the hill towards the farm, her brother decided to make several faces at her from behind.

Aleksander had been working more diligently than usual to accomplish his chores that day. He didn't want to bore Liliana by having her sit and wait while he finished cleaning the stalls. After he finished the last stall, he went to wash his hands profusely before going to take a quick bath.

"Hello?" He heard from outside the barn. Liliana was here.

Aleksander clicked his tongue, which he often did

when he was frustrated. He quickly weighed the options of asking Liliana to wait while he bathed or just going without a bath altogether.

He went with the latter, feeling that a bath just might take too long.

Making sure his hands were extra clean, he walked out of the barn to meet his guests. Liliana and, from what Aleksander could guess, her little brother were both aimlessly walking around the outer fence to the Kurtz farm.

"Good afternoon, Miss Hodor," Aleksander greeted as he approached them.

"Liliana is fine, Aleksander," Liliana dismissed with a wave. Then she gestured to her brother. "This is my brother, Albin."

"Good afternoon, Mr. Hodor." Aleksander nodded with a gentle smile.

"Aleksander, please," Liliana laughed. "Just call him Albin."

"No, Mr. Hodor is fine." Albin grinned, folding his arms proudly.

Aleksander returned Albin's grin. He had done well with a first impression for Liliana's brother.

"Can we see the horses?" Liliana got straight to the point. Her excitement was palpable.

"Of course," Aleksander replied.

Liliana's expectations were quite unmet when she realized that Aleksander did not operate by the traditional methods she had read about. Aleksander had gone to the barn where the horses were kept and simply unlocked one horse's stall, whistling to him to follow after. And the horse did.

"This is Kasper," Aleksander introduced as he called Kasper to him. The horse obediently walked over to Aleksander.

"Kasper, this is Liliana and Albin," Aleksander told the horse. "Say hello."

Kasper, looking over at Liliana and Albin, suddenly bowed forward on his front right leg, kneeling on his front left leg. The horse's face nearly touched the ground, he bowed so low. Liliana never knew a horse could do something so elegant and noble-looking.

"Ohhh, he's amazing," Liliana cooed at Kasper. Aleksander smiled. This was going very well for him. Thanks to Kasper, Liliana would hardly forget him now. "Good boy." Aleksander offered some oats to Kasper.

Kasper stood up from his bow and greedily consumed the oats. Aleksander then gently stroked the horse's neck when suddenly Kasper nipped at Aleksander's hair playfully.

"Hey, stop that," Aleksander laughed as he shooed the horse's face away. Kasper lifted his head away from Aleksander's, still having a very playful aura about him. Liliana raised her eyebrows in surprise. Something that was happening more and more around Aleksander.

"They look like friends." Liliana pieced together. *"Not horse and master."*

All the same, Liliana found herself smiling warmly at it. It was much more wonderful to see a bond of friendship between a boy and his horse than a master and slave kind of relationship.

"Would you like to go for a simple ride?" Aleksander offered. "Nothing crazy. Just a slow walking speed."

"YES!" Liliana cheered.

Kasper was saddled, and Aleksander walked Liliana through some basics of mounting on the horse. "Always get on the horse from the horse's left side," he instructed.

"Why?" Albin asked as Liliana approached Kasper on his left side.

"I'm not sure why." Aleksander shrugged at Albin. "But it's the way we've always done it here, so it will let the horse know ahead of time to prepare their balance for the rider."

"Makes sense." Albin nodded.

Aleksander then placed a sturdy bucket between Liliana and Kasper.

"You can use that to help with his height." Aleksander pointed to the bucket. Liliana got up on the bucket. "Now, left foot in the stirrup," Aleksander told her, "And then swing your right leg over the horse and sit tall in the saddle."

Liliana obeyed. Kasper cooperated with her without any issues. Aleksander knew he would, being one of the gentler horses.

"Good," Aleksander praised.

Liliana took the reins in her hands. "Okay, I'm ready for the next step."

Aleksander walked up beside Kasper and quickly

25

took the reins from Liliana's hands. "No. You're inexperienced." Then, with the reins in his hand, Aleksander began leading Kasper along while Liliana sat on top.

Liliana furrowed her brow. That was it? Being led around on a horse like a child at a fair? Sure, it was exciting to be up close to a horse and even be able to be on that horse.

However, the initial excitement had almost altogether faded after just a few seconds of being led around by Aleksander. What good was it to be able to ride a horse if Liliana wasn't able to *really* ride? Just trudging along at an unbearably slow walk? There was no thrill to that.

So, Liliana conceived a mischievous plan as she threw off her hat.

"Aleksander." She called. Aleksander turned to look at her.

"The wind blew my hat off." She pointed off towards the hat. Luckily enough for her, the wind actually did pick up a bit, and the hat was carried a few yards off.

"Would you mind fetching it for me?" Liliana asked, giving Aleksander her signature doe eyes.

Aleksander paused as he watched the hat gently fall to the ground. Then, his eyes turned back to Liliana.

Liliana got the sense that Aleksander was cautious to let go of the horse's reins with her being a brand-new rider.

"Don't worry!" She laughed innocently. "I'll be

fine! It'll just be a second!"

Aleksander hesitated a second more before nodding and jogging off to get the hat.

Liliana's innocence melted away as she snatched the loose reins and gripped them tightly. She snapped the reins.

Kasper did nothing.

"What?" She huffed, confused. "I'm sure that's what you're supposed to do…Oh, wait!"

She took both of her heels and dug them sharply into Kasper's side.

That was it. The horse instantly lunged forward. "Liliana!" Aleksander shouted as the girl sped off on the horse.

Liliana was instantly in a panic. It was a miracle that she had not flipped off the back of the horse. The only thing that saved her at that moment was grabbing hold of the horse's mane.

Needless to say, she had not expected this. The horse had gone from a simple walk to the speed of a bullet. The initial whiplash she suffered instantly brought pain to her back, waist, and neck. Furthermore, everything she had thought of horse galloping was wrong. She thought it would be like riding a motorcycle. Fast, absolutely, but also a sense of smoothness and at least a tiny sense of security.

The horse was not smooth like a motorcycle. The horse had legs, not wheels. With each gallop, Liliana was jerked and jolted around terribly. She imagined it wasn't unlike being in a devastating earthquake. Only this earthquake was also flying.

When it came to security, the only sense of security Liliana had was simply holding onto the horse for dear life. There was no safety harness. There was no seatbelt. There was nothing but her own hands to hold on to the horse's mane, and her own legs to hold onto the horse.

It was absolutely terrifying.

"This was a mistake!" Liliana screamed as she hoped that she would not fly off the horse. "A very horrible mistake!" She knew that the chances of Aleksander or Albin catching up to her were slim to none. And though Liliana believed in God (and was frantically praying to Him in that moment), she knew that God was not always eager to save fools from their own stupidity.

It was up to her to save herself.

"The reins!" She realized after racking her brain on how to stop a rampaging horse. In order to stop the horse, she needed to pull back on the reins. The reins were currently flapping in the wind. Liliana mustered up her courage to release one hand from the horse's mane and snatched the reins out of the air.

Then she pulled back with all of her might.

Another mistake she came to find. She had pulled back too much on the reins. The bit in the horse's mouth was jerked back too violently, causing Kasper's mouth to bleed.

This frightened the horse, which made him charge forward even faster. What was worse, Liliana lost hold of the reins again and was too afraid of letting go of Kasper's mane to try and get them back again.

"I'm dead," Liliana concluded as she stiffly held her death grip on the horse.

But as Kasper continued racing down the path, Liliana realized that remaining stiff was making her bounce around all the worse. Loosening up only slightly in her lower back, as she tried to move with the horse, she found it wasn't as painful, and it wasn't as scary. Growing more confident, she sat up more in the saddle but still made sure to lean forward. She still held on tightly but was starting to feel more in control. As she did, she was beginning to understand the kind of exhilaration it was to ride at full gallop. It wasn't like a vehicle. It was unique. It felt more alive.

Just as Liliana was beginning to relish her riding experience, sounds of hooves came surging up beside her. Aleksander was on a different horse, expertly riding up alongside Kasper and Liliana. With a look that could kill, he seized Kasper's reins and began to gradually slow Kasper down.

"Whoa! Whoa," he called to Kasper as the two riders began coming to a stop.

"I'm in trouble." Liliana knew.

But she always had a way of getting herself back out of trouble.

"I'm sorry." Liliana smiled as she batted her eyes at Aleksander. "I just couldn't help myself."

Liliana knew that no one could resist forgiving her the moment she poured on the sweet attitude. She had gotten in trouble plenty of times. With her father, with her teacher, with past boyfriends. And, sure as the sunrise, the moment she tossed her hair and pleaded with her eyes, she would get away with almost anything. Putting on a child-like innocence, partnered with her beauty, was guaranteed to work on any man.

...But Aleksander's fierce gaze didn't falter.

"It was just a bit of fun," Liliana added, thinking it would just take another push. "No one was hurt."

If anything, Aleksander looked even angrier.

"Get off my horse," he growled at her.

There was an intimidating, but restrained power behind Aleksander's voice. The kind that made people understand that the situation was serious. The kind that made people obey without question.

Which is exactly what Liliana did.

She dismounted the horse quickly, slightly afraid of what Aleksander might do. She knew, after all, that this boy was capable of significant feats of strength. She, nor her brother (who was still trying to catch up to where the other two were), would be any match for an angry Aleksander.

But after Liliana dismounted, she found that Aleksander had already dismounted his horse as well. He had gone to Liliana's horse and began softly stroking the horse's neck, making calming, soothing sounds to the magnificent beast. Liliana then noticed that Kasper still seemed unsettled.

Breathing hard and having a bit of a frightened look in his eyes—it was also then that she saw the blood in the horse's mouth for the first time.

"You startled him," Aleksander fumed, not even

looking at Liliana. "You **hurt** him."

"I—I'm sorry," Liliana stuttered, her apology much more real now. "I...I just—"

"These are powerful animals." Aleksander finally turned to face Liliana. "Capable of **killing** you, Liliana. What you did was extremely reckless."

Aleksander's initial anger was almost gone entirely. A remnant of it still burned in his eyes, but it was under control. Instead of the furious growl he had spoken in just moments ago, it was replaced with a calm, patient, but stern voice.

Liliana found herself no longer afraid of Aleksander. Just ashamed.

Aleksander was right. Liliana had no experience riding a horse. Considering what all could have happened, her little rebellious ride had gone extremely well. After all, Kasper could have easily bucked her off and even trampled over her. Who knows what could have taken place?

Liliana bowed her head. "I'm sorry. I'm truly sorry."

"I forgive you," Aleksander replied immediately.

Liliana lifted her head. "You do?"

"Yes." Aleksander nodded, giving a hint of a smile. "In time, you can get experienced enough to be able to ride at a gallop like that, but that takes patience."

Suddenly, Aleksander held out Liliana's hat to her. She hadn't even realized that he had held onto it this entire time.

"That being said, you did rather well for a

beginner," Aleksander mentioned as Liliana took back her hat.

"Thank you," she muttered softly.

"I think that's enough for today," Aleksander told her as her brother finally came running over the hill to catch up to them. "It's been a bit more exciting than I hoped for." Liliana's heart sank, knowing Aleksander was subtly telling her to leave and not come back. Her foolish behavior had cost her future experiences with horses.

At least, that's what she thought until Aleksander asked, "Would you like to come by sometime next week?"

Liliana was somewhat shocked to still be invited to come back. "I would, yes."

"We can discuss what day is best when at school." Aleksander nodded.

Liliana thought about the encounter as she and her brother were walking home. Aleksander was a peculiar individual to her. He did not follow the domineering protocol that she had read so much about. Instead, he had treated his horses with respect, trust, and kindness. This was added to a growing pile of peculiarities surrounding the boy. Small, but strong. Quiet, but considerate. Firm, but kind.

"You got him really angry." Her brother brought up, bringing Liliana back from her thoughts.

"Yes..." Liliana agreed with a touch of shame on her face. "Yes, I did."

32

"You should have seen his face when you first took off." He laughed. "I thought he was ready to strangle you. Did you do your batting eyes trick on him?"

"Yes," Liliana recalled with some surprise, "but he didn't fall for it."

"Is that a good thing or a bad thing?" Her brother questioned.

Liliana shrugged. "I'm not sure. I suppose I'll either have to come up with new tricks or just be real with him."

CHAPTER THREE:

Tomasz

Tomasz Kurtz watched his son and his new friends from inside their humble house. It would seem that Aleksander was trying to impress a pretty girl with a riding lesson. Tomasz chuckled to himself before releasing a tantrum of coughing.

"The horses," he sputtered to himself as the coughing subsided. "The ladies always love the horses."

It was how Tomasz had first gotten the notice of Aleksander's mother, Krystyna. Like Aleksander, Tomasz had tended to horses when he was a boy. He was the youngest of four. He had been the most athletic and the most energetic. He used to try and get Krystyna's attention by doing dangerous trick riding while on horseback. But that young man was long gone...

Though he endeavored to be a gentle, patient, kind man, he now held a great deal of care beneath his wrinkled brow. He looked a great deal older than he truly was. The War to End All Wars ensured that.

Tomasz Kurtz was called into battle, along with his two brothers, in late 1914. His brothers never made it through. Tomasz himself almost didn't. One day, the three brothers were all sitting in their trench, alive and well...

The next? Just one artillery shell of mustard gas

changed all of that. Tomasz's brothers didn't get their masks on in time. Tomasz barely did, but not without consequence. He was hospitalized and he "recovered," but he was never the same.

A vicious, chronic cough was a constant part of his life now. Every time he broke into his fit of hacking, it felt like someone was hitting him in the chest with a hammer.

But he made do. God had brought him through that terror. He had gone back to Krystyna and asked her to marry him, and much to his surprise, she said yes.

Tomasz sighed, sadly longing for his departed wife.

Aleksander hadn't even reached a year old before the Lord called Krystyna home. How strange it was that Tomasz had outlasted her. To be honest, though, he preferred it.

Krystyna was now in a place of eternal peace and rest while Tomasz plodded on in the hard, dark times that Earth provided. He was thankful that Krystyna did not have to be left alone in the suffering that he felt.

...Or left with the finances, for that matter.

Tomasz despised budgeting, for he always knew the end balance would be less than desired. War had scarred Europe, and many people were not doing well financially. It was a miracle alone that Tomasz was able to get his son into school. After all, he wanted his son to have a chance to be much more educated than he was. Mathematics and finances were a struggle for Tomasz, and he wanted to ensure that Aleksander would not one day grow to have those same issues.

"If only I had listened to Nina," Tomasz thought with a small chuckle as he tapped a letter that was on his desk. Nina, Tomasz's sister. His only living sibling. After the war, she had decided to go to America with her husband. A bold move, but apparently a very fruitful one. Nina had written to Tomasz a while back about how the country was doing very well, albeit mostly financially. Spiritually? Not so much. This was why Tomasz refrained from giving his sister a straight answer when she would ask if he would move to America as well.

A new country, a new language, a new culture, a new occupation…those were all hard enough. But all of that, mixed with the fact that America was not seeking the things of God? No, that was not what he wanted for himself or his son.

Glancing around the house, deep in thought, Tomasz had to admit that things didn't seem the best of circumstances in Europe, either. Poland's neighbor, Germany, had naught but ominous and frightening news of late. A man known as Adolf Hitler was becoming quite the talk of the political realm. He had recently become the chancellor of Germany, which worried Tomasz. This Hitler was a radical who had been sentenced to prison for high treason only ten years ago. Now, he was loose and in power with his extreme ideologies. Tomasz had heard of Chancellor Hitler's book, *Mein Kampf*, and how Hitler spoke of the Jewish people as being altogether evil.

"Haman's spirit follows us to the twentieth century..." Tomasz spoke out loud with a grumble.

Tomasz was a Jewish man, as was Aleksander, though they followed the teachings of Jesus Christ, thereby being Christians. But when it came to blood, they could be traced back to Abraham.

Amid budgeting finances and dwelling on politics, Tomasz drifted off. His dream began pleasantly as he found himself riding a horse at full gallop. Horseback riding was no longer permitted to Tomasz. At least not that kind. Anything too exciting could throw him into a coughing fit, and Aleksander worried too much about his father to risk him on the back of an animal while hacking away. If anything, Tomasz was allowed slow or gentle rides.

But here, Tomasz was riding like he had before the war. Doing tricks to impress Krystyna. Laughing. Taunting his brothers.

But good dreams don't always last. Tomasz found a mustard-yellow gas started seeping at the horse's feet. He urged the horse in the opposite direction but found that he was suddenly in No-Man's Land. Gunshots and mortars were sounding everywhere. The horse itself suddenly bucked and knocked Tomasz clean off. Falling in the putrid mud, Tomasz did his best to get up.

Suddenly, Tomasz saw a man towering over him, putting a rifle in his face. The man cocked the rifle, ready to shoot. Tomasz instinctively threw the hardest punch he could.

Aleksander reacted instantly, parrying his father's strike so that Tomasz's fist missed Aleksander's face by a mere few inches.

"Father!" Aleksander shouted.

Aleksander's voice brought Tomasz back. He immediately recoiled his fist, looking at his son in alarm and guilt. "Aleksander!" He realized, only whispering his name.

Tomasz frantically looked around to see if the intruder was still on the premises. Where was the gunfire? The stinking wasteland? The barbed wire and explosions?

No, he was safe. He was in his house. The war was long over. Only a memory mingled with a nightmare.

Then, as sweat continued pouring down his face, Tomasz turned a worried face back to Aleksander. "Oh, son, I didn't hurt you, did I?"

"No, sir." Aleksander calmed and stood in a casual stance. Tomasz analyzed his son closely to make sure Aleksander was being honest. When it came to Tomasz, Aleksander had a nasty habit of lying in order to make his father feel better.

But gazing carefully at the strong young man proved that Aleksander was unharmed. Tomasz couldn't help but grin. It would take a lot more than an old veteran to be able to lay a hand on that youth.

"I taught you well, boy." Tomasz couldn't help but be proud of his son. "You tossed my fist away like it was chaff on the wind."

Aleksander allowed himself a small, quiet smile at that. "Not that I'm Samson or anything." Tomasz began joking. But as soon as he did, the coughing returned. His lungs began squeezing, feeling like they might turn inside out.

Aleksander gazed upon his father with a mournful somberness. Lately, his father seemed to be getting worse, coughing more frequently and bringing up excess mucus.

It wasn't blood, which was a good sign, but Tomasz's condition affected his physical prowess more and more every year, it seemed. Without a word, Aleksander moved to the windows around the house and opened all of them. The doctor had instructed Tomaz to get as much fresh air as possible.

Aleksander also silently swept the house for his father's secret stash of cigarettes, knowing that his father's condition worsened exceedingly after a smoke break.

Tomasz reasoned that the smoking calmed him, but Aleksander could easily observe that whatever benefit the cigarettes brought, the ill consequences weighed far more. Finding a small box hidden underneath the bed, Aleksander quickly and quietly disposed of it outside, retrieved some water from the pump, and returned to his father with a cup of water.

"Thank you, boy," Tomasz praised him warmly after he recovered from his coughing. He drank heartily as Aleksander continued to stand silent in his presence.

"By the way, where did you run off to the other day?" Tomasz asked. "You were out very late."

"Forgive me, sir," Aleksander apologized. "I was repairing a bench."

"Hm," Tomasz responded before glancing out the window. "So...you had some friends over?"

"Yes, sir."

Tomasz then eyed his son with a knowing look. "And that girl. Liliana Hodor?"

Aleksander took an uneasy breath. "Yes, sir."

"Hmm..." Tomasz hummed as he stroked his beard. "What are your intentions?"

"Currently, to get to know her better, sir," Aleksander answered.

"And after you know her better?" Tomasz questioned.

Aleksander paused before answering. "With all hope and prayer...I thought I might ask her parents for their blessing and you for yours."

"To court her?"

"Yes, sir."

"So, you're serious about her?" Tomasz asked, somewhat surprised. "What makes her so special?"

Aleksander didn't answer.

"You don't know?" Tomasz pressed.

"I...I find her pretty, sir." Aleksander answered with a hint of shame, knowing it wasn't a good enough answer. Aleksander then remembered something else. "And—and she was kind to me. Not everyone is."

"A godly bride is much more than a pretty face

and kind treatment," Tomasz instructed. "I praise your caution in simply becoming friends first, but beware that heart of yours. It will want to take leaps and bounds, where God says to just take one step at a time. You remember Jeremiah 17:5-9?"

"'Thus said the LORD; Cursed be the man that trusteth in man, and maketh flesh his arm, and whose heart departeth from the Lord.'" Aleksander quoted. "'For he shall be like the heath in the desert, and shall not see when good cometh; but shall inhabit the parched places in the wilderness, in a salt land and not inhabited. Blessed is the man that trusteth in the Lord, and whose hope the Lord is. For he shall be as a tree planted by the waters, and that spreadeth out her roots by the river, and shall not see when heat cometh, but her leaf shall be green; and shall not be careful in the year of drought, neither shall cease from yielding fruit. The heart is deceitful above all things, and desperately wicked: who can know it?'"

"Good. Good." Tomasz nodded approvingly. "And the Proverbs of Solomon? Proverbs 4:23-27?"

"Keep thy heart with all diligence; for out of it are the issues of life. Put away from thee a froward mouth, and perverse lips put far from thee. Let thine eyes look right on, and let thine eyelids look straight before thee. Ponder the path of thy feet, and let all thy ways be established. Turn not to the right hand nor to the left: remove thy foot from evil.'"

"It all starts with the heart, boy," Tomasz said as he continued to nod. "The heart will affect the lips and the eyes. The eyes will affect your feet. The musings in your heart will determine what path your feet trod. Satan will seek to drive your heart down the wrong path, and he might use this girl to do it. Keep your heart."

"Yes, sir."

"Meditate on those verses while around her." Tomasz leaned forward and tapped a finger on Aleksander's chest. "And when you're not around her, pray for guidance. If you truly seek the Lord's will, He'll make it known to you *and* me."

"You, sir?"

"The best sign the Lord can give you that He approves of this girl is by telling me first." Tomasz smiled. "That's not in the Bible, but that's what my father told me, and sure enough, it happened when I brought your mother to him. Trust me, I'm looking out for you."

Aleksander smiled at Tomasz. "I trust you more than anyone, Father."

Tomasz beamed. "You're a good son. Horses all taken care of?"

"Yes, sir."

"Other animals?"

"Yes, sir."

"Good job." Tomasz pointed to the pump outside. "Go wash up. I'll have dinner on soon."

Aleksander obeyed immediately, heading to the door. "And, son," Tomasz called.

Aleksander stopped and turned back to his father. Tomasz suppressed a grin. "You told her about the horses on purpose, didn't you? You knew that'd hook her, didn't you?"

Aleksander simply smiled in response before heading out to the water pump.

CHAPTER FOUR:

A Connection

"Tell us!" One of Liliana's friends pressed her. "What happened? Are you two an item? Is that why Aleksander fought Piotr?"

"An item? Certainly not." Liliana scoffed. "I don't think that's even his intention."

Liliana had made an effort to spend time with her friends after school at least once a week. The week after she had gone to Aleksander's, it seemed that news had already spread of her time on the Kurtz farm.

"What else would his intentions be?" One of the girls answered Liliana. "And, more importantly, what are *yours?* Albin told my brother that you two walked all the way to his father's farm."

"Yes, because he has horses," Liliana reasoned. "And I got to ride one. I was told that I was already basically an expert!"

"Naturally, for you." One praised.

"I know," Liliana boasted. "First time, too."

"But what about Aleksander?"

"What *about* Aleksander?" Liliana replied.

"What's he really like?" She questioned. "And does he have eyes for you?"

"Is that why he fought Piotr?" Another interjected. One of the girls gasped. "A battle of jealousy! They're fighting for her hand!"

"Calm down, now," Liliana told them, gently. "There's nothing between me and either of those boys."

But it was too late. The girls had gotten too excited and began frantically talking among themselves about Liliana's supposed love life with Aleksander. They weren't even listening to her now.

"I have to nip this in the bud." Liliana worried as she witnessed them all chattering about. She knew the relationship rumor mill ate up any juicy story it could find, and her friends, love them as she might, were not the best at keeping secrets. From this, Liliana imagined, with horror, what life would be like if people thought she and Aleksander were a romantic couple.

"Aleksander is a decent person," Liliana proclaimed loudly so she could be heard above all of the girls. They quickly silenced as she spoke. "But we aren't even friends, really. I don't like him like that, and he certainly doesn't have eyes for me. We're more like acquaintances with similar interests."

"Similar interests?" One girl queried.

"Well, similar interest." Liliana corrected. "Horses."

"How can you be sure he doesn't have a candle lit for you?" Another one brought up.

Liliana turned her eyes away from them, a hair embarrassed. "I...may have made him rather angry." The girls leaned in, eager for the rest of the story.

Liliana sighed. "I hurt one of his horses." Her

friends gasped in alarm.

"It was bad," Liliana admitted. "And I've never seen him so angry before."

"Did he hurt you?"

"Threaten you?"

"What? No," Liliana dismissed immediately. "I told you, he's decent."

"What did he say?"

"He asked me to leave," Liliana admitted ashamedly. "I apologized, and everything is fine now. But he *clearly* has no intention to court a girl like me."

"You intend to court my sister, don't you?" Albin asked Aleksander as Liliana gently walked Kasper about. Thankfully, Liliana was just out of earshot, and Aleksander gave Albin a look that told the boy everything.

Albin nodded knowingly. "Don't worry. I won't tell."

Aleksander paused. "…Why would I be worried about you telling? I'm not trying to hide that fact."

"Believe me, you want to hide that for now," Albin advised. "Liliana thinks you're fine, but the instant she finds out you want to be her new love interest, she'll run away from you."

"Am I that despicable?" Aleksander deflated.

"No," Albin answered. "She just doesn't know what's good for her. I like you, actually. You're not a lunkhead who falls for my sister's tricks or does anything and everything to make her happy. And, in time, Liliana will learn to like you, too. Right now, she's just not sure about you."

Aleksander creased his brow. "I never saw her as someone so...self-centered."

Albin shrugged. "She's not the worst person around. Believe me, she really is a nice girl." Albin paused. "Don't tell her I said that."

"Your secret is safe," Aleksander replied.

"Good," Albin sighed with relief. "But, anyway, she is smart, kind, decent, and pretty much everything you already think. The problem is that she's been told that so much that she's gotten in her mind that she's basically perfect. The horde of friends that she has doesn't help it, either. They basically worship her. So now, Liliana likes being able to get what she wants. Father wants her to move past that, but it's hung on for a bit longer than he thought it would."

Aleksander blinked at Albin. "How old are you?"

"Sound older than my age, eh?" Albin asked proudly. "In truth, I'm eleven. I've been exposed to a great deal of drama due to Liliana, though. I'm something of a relationship expert now."

"Are you now?" Aleksander couldn't help but grin. "Then riddle me this: what should I do to convince your sister not to run away when she finds out I like her?"

"Nothing," Albin asserted firmly. "Don't try and be something you're not. Don't bend over backward for her. Don't be a dog that will roll over for her.

47

Don't stoop to those levels. Be who you are and open her eyes. Show her what a man is among boys."

Then Albin thought a bit more. "And pray. You'll definitely need God to slap her upside the head to see straight."

Aleksander gave a small laugh. "I'll keep that in mind."

"Good." Albin folded his arms. "That way, you can get her to stop complaining at home. I long for a day when she's not wailing about boys and love."

Aleksander snorted at that.

Albin and Liliana's visits became quite a regular occurrence. As the riding lessons continued, the two Hodors became quite skilled around horses. Albin and Aleksander also became like brothers. After all, neither boy had any brothers. And, just like Albin had told Aleksander, Liliana began to see Aleksander as something different. Not yet a man she could have a relationship with, but he was now much more than the odd kid at school.

"How long have you ridden horses, Aleksander?" Liliana asked as the three rode together.

Albin glanced over at his sister and very subtly began slowing his horse down to fall behind Aleksander and Liliana. Albin sensed this was a good opportunity for the two to feel alone, even though they weren't.

Aleksander considered the question. "I've been on a horse since before I could walk. My father tells me

48

that my first ride was with my mother."

Liliana paused at that, another question arising in her mind. "I…"

Then, she stopped, fearing the question would be too brazen to ask.

Aleksander glanced at her. "Yes?"

"Well, it's a rather personal question," Liliana muttered.

"You can ask," Aleksander told her. "I don't mind."

"Your mother…" Liliana put it delicately. Then, she shook her head. "No, forget I said anything. I shouldn't ask about such things. Forget I said anything."

There was a pause between the two as only the sound of horse hooves rang out.

"Tuberculosis," Aleksander answered.

"What?" Liliana questioned.

"You wanted to know how she died." Aleksander guessed. "She died of tuberculosis."

"Oh…Oh, I'm sorry."

"I wouldn't worry." Aleksander tried to reassure her. "I was very young when it happened. I don't remember her."

"Still…" Liliana murmured sorrowfully. "It's quite a tragedy."

"I will meet her someday." Aleksander smiled, glancing up at the sky.

Liliana followed suit, looking up towards the clouds. "You really are very religious."

"My God saved me from my sins." Aleksander

pointed out. "He didn't have to, and therefore I am extremely grateful. The least I can do for Him is honor Him for His great and wondrous works."

Liliana stared at Aleksander. "You make me feel guilty."

"Why?" Aleksander looked surprised.

"Well, I'm a Christian, too," Liliana mentioned.

"Are you?" Aleksander was delighted. "Wonderful!"

"Well, yeah, but you're…" Liliana muttered, somewhat frustrated. "You're a much more spiritual Christian than I am, and it makes me feel guilty."

"Guilt is how God speaks to us sometimes," Aleksander replied poetically. "The next step would be to find out why the guilt is there, and then take care of it."

"Hmm…" Liliana responded uncertainly.

"I've always found prayer to be the best way to clear things up between God and me," Aleksander continued. "Prayer is like drawing closer to a fire on a winter's night. The closer you get, the more the iciness melts away and the more the warmth of God's compassion surrounds you."

Liliana considered Aleksander's words that night while lying in bed.

Liliana's family was religious. They went to church, read the Bible together, prayed together, and did all the things that good Christians were supposed to do. Liliana's father often stated how God had

50

greatly blessed their family and his business. But lately, Liliana had found God rather more like a nuisance. It was a bother to get up early on Sundays for church. It was annoying to have to go through a Bible that spoke in such an old language. God was a distraction that was keeping her from her friends and her fun.

That being said, she had moments where she felt the stinging guilt of neglecting God after all God had done for her. But the more she ignored that guilt, the less and less it stung, and the less and less it came around.

Until she began hanging around Aleksander.

Aleksander was a constant reminder of everything Christian. When he spoke, he mentioned Jesus often. He talked about Bible passages he was going through. And he wouldn't stop talking about how vital prayer was.

Liliana concentrated as she tried to remember the last time she had prayed an authentic prayer rather than the memorized jargon she had tended to do lately.

She couldn't remember the last time…

So, with the guilt welling up inside her, she threw off her covers and knelt beside her bed. She prayed to her Lord. Not the rehearsed, repeated prayer. No, this time she prayed genuinely. And, unbeknownst to her, her father heard her outside of her room.

CHAPTER FIVE:

Fathers

A knock came to Tomasz's front door one afternoon. Tomasz hesitated, an anxious uncertainty arising in him. Aleksander never knocked. Why would he? And Tomasz wasn't expecting anyone either.

Taking a deep breath, Tomasz's hand slowly moved and hovered over the pistol he kept on his person.

"Yes?" Tomasz spoke, holding back a cough. "Who's there?"

"Mr. Kurtz?" A man called from the other side of the door. "It's Jozef Hodor. Liliana's father."

"Jozef Hodor," Tomasz sighed to himself, allowing himself to ease up. Tomasz coughed some as he stood up and went to unlock the front door.

"How may I help you today, Mr. Hodor?" Tomasz smiled politely at the man who stood on his porch.

Jozef smiled back. "Is Aleksander here?"

"No, not presently."

"Good." Jozef nodded a few times. "May I speak with you?"

"Of course, come in. Come in." Tomasz beckoned, letting Jozef inside.

Jozef Hodor was a businessman. He owned a construction business that was vitally needed after the conclusion of the war. Poland, though not an independent state during the war, had suffered much damage. Jozef Hodor was one of the many people who sought to rebuild their country, and he had become quite wealthy because of it. In that, Tomasz found himself slightly envious of Jozef. Of course, Tomasz knew that wealth brought its own problems, but they seemed to be less burdensome than the problems that came with poverty.

Other than Jozef's business, Tomasz didn't know much about the man.

"Would you like anything to drink?" Tomasz offered. "Any food, perhaps?"

"No, no, sir," Jozef politely refused. "I just wish to have a quiet discussion with you, if I may."

Tomasz sat down, feeling slightly uneasy. "Has Aleksander done something?"

Jozef let a smile manifest. "Well, yes, I suppose he has." Tomasz waited for Jozef to clarify.

"He's influencing my daughter," Jozef said in a pleased tone, "and my son, Albin, for that matter. But I haven't been too worried about Albin lately. Liliana, on the other hand…"

He let the sentence trail off.

"Forgive me, Mr. Hodor," Tomasz scoffed, growing tired of the vague speech, "but get to it. What are you trying to say?"

Jozef drew in a breath. "Your son invited my children to come to this farm and be taught horse riding lessons, Mr. Kurtz. You're aware of this?"

"Yes," Tomasz answered. "Were you not?"

"No, my daughter told me right away and asked

my permission. I told her that would be fine." Jozef explained. "I suspected it was another boy's ploy at impressing my daughter in hopes of eventually dating her."

"Aleksander does have that hope," Tomasz confessed.

"Yes, Albin told me." Jozef nodded. "The thing is, he's quite different from other young men I've observed. Plainly speaking, my daughter is…spoiled. She has an air of entitlement about her and wishes to always get her way. But since she's been coming here, I've been noticing a change in her."

"A good one, I hope," Tomasz said.

"Yes," Jozef answered. "More humble, obedient, and diligent, I've found. She attends to her Bible more, and I've even found her praying again."

Tomasz allowed a proud smile to show. "I'm glad to hear this, Mr. Hodor. I must say, though, I'm still not sure where this is going. You came all this way to tell me this?"

"I came to ask you what your son intends." Jozef finally spit it out. "This all seems wonderful to me, but I'm worried that this is merely a ploy to look good to me. You know of my family's wealth."

Tomasz waved his hand dismissively. "Your wealth matters very little to Aleksander. But why trust me? I'm the boy's father. I could tell you anything just to make Aleksander look good."

"I may not know you well, but I know of you. Everyone who speaks of you speaks well of you." Jozef pointed at Tomasz. "And you're right. You are his father. You know what it's like to hold that little baby in your arms and pray to the Lord that they do things right in life. That you lead them right, so they don't make a monumental mess of their life. I doubt you want your son to be in a relationship with my daughter if he's scheming about."

Tomasz thought about Jozef's words.

"Wisely put, sir." Then, Tomasz stood to his feet. "Let's walk."

Tomasz led Jozef outside to the hill that overlooked the entire farm.

"We have a good number of animals here." Tomasz began pointing from building to building. "No hogs, of course, but dairy cows, a few beef cattle, chickens, horses." He then glanced at Jozef. "Aleksander manages them all. I do very, very little. I do the business side of things. Purchasing, selling, things such as that. But Aleksander? He tends to the animals, feeds them, manages their coops and stables, everything."

Jozef took this in as he gazed over the farm.

"Your daughter will tell you that Aleksander has a way with the horses, too." Tomasz continued. "Not the traditional way. He's kind and compassionate to them. Treats them with respect and trust."

Tomasz suddenly went into one of his fits of coughing. He hacked for several minutes while Jozef repeatedly asked if he was all right.

"I'm fine, I'm fine," Tomasz reassured him as he recovered. "One of my…conditions from the war." Jozef understood immediately. He had been in the war himself.

"It's getting worse," Tomasz admitted. "But Aleksander takes care of everything to make sure I get the rest I need. And he's very proud of who I am, not that he should be. But the boy trains himself when he's not busy. He wishes to be strong like I was before the war. He has a deep desire to protect those he cares about."

Tomasz then looked Jozef in the eyes. "So, let the boy's work tell you what you need to know about him."

Jozef considered this. From what he could see from the farm, it was in fair condition. The only glaring thing was the obvious sign of wear that the buildings had due to time and use. Every other aspect was in order and good shape.

"Hardworking." Jozef listed in his mind. *"Organized."* Liliana and Albin both had mentioned Aleksander's care of the horses and how he managed them in a way that was different than most.

"Kind." Jozef continued listing. *"Gentle."* Lastly, Jozef analyzed Tomasz himself and how violently the man had coughed just moments ago.

"Clearly the mustard gas…" Jozef knew. But Jozef also knew that men with such conditions typically didn't last as long as Tomasz had. That meant that either Tomasz was lucky, or that Aleksander cared for his father so well that Tomasz's condition had not yet worsened as much as it usually did.

"A provider." Jozef checked off his mental list.

56

"And, if Tomasz is being honest, a protector." The two men shook hands, and Jozef began his drive back home.

"An individual who meets many of my requirements," Jozef noted. *"He might, in fact, be the right young man. I'm rather excited to meet him."*

Back at the Kurtz residence, Aleksander returned from doing his daily workout routine. He found his father in a surprisingly happy mood.

"Did I miss something?" Aleksander asked his father.

"Nothing the Lord didn't want you to miss." Tomasz grinned as he replied.

CHAPTER SIX:
The Question

It was time. Aleksander and Liliana had been meeting almost every week for the past three months. It was true that Liliana had lost some of the initial shine that Aleksander had seen before he got to know her. He was grateful he came to know more about who she was before actively trying to pursue her. Furthermore, Aleksander prayed earnestly that God would show him if Liliana was the right one for him, or, more importantly, if he was the right one for her.

Aleksander was given no obvious sign that Liliana wasn't right for him. And Aleksander still nurtured feelings for the girl. In fact, after coming to befriend her, he felt his affection for her had grown even more.

It was time for the question.

"Father." Aleksander approached Tomasz, who was smoking outside on the hill.

Aleksander kicked himself inwardly, making his signature *"tch"* sound as he realized he had not found every stash of his father's cigarettes.

"Hm?" Tomasz turned to Aleksander.

"Three and a half months ago, we spoke of Liliana Hodor," Aleksander began, "and you asked me what my intentions were concerning her."

Tomasz put out his cigarette, making the connection that this was going to be a rather important conversation.

"I told you that I wished to get to know her better, and I have," Aleksander continued. "My feelings for her have not changed. In fact, they have grown. She's more than a pretty face and a kind person. She is a Christian woman who, admittedly, has not always put Christ first in her life. However, we have been discussing the Bible lately, and she tells me that I have encouraged her to get right with God and start being more faithful in all things that are godly. I have been praying earnestly about this, and I don't believe I've received a 'no' from God. But I also prayed that God might speak through you."

Aleksander nearly snapped to attention. "Sir, do I have your blessing to ask Liliana Hodor if I may court her? Whatever your decision, I will heartily obey."

Tomasz allowed a warm smile. "I'm proud of you, son. I do believe that God is telling me that this is a good path for you to travel down. Now, you two aren't married, so don't get the idea that she's the one for you. This is just a stepping stone to finding out that answer. But, to answer your question, I do give my blessing, so long as her father does as well. What did he say?"

Aleksander stood completely still, not answering a word. Tomasz's smile vanished, and a frown replaced it. "You did ask him, too, didn't you?"

"Well..." Aleksander began.

"Aleksander," Tomasz scolded. "You know, I thought it was odd that Liliana's father was here the other day. He told me that you've never spoken to him. Is that still the case?"

"I've not spoken to him yet, sir," Aleksander admitted.

"Why not?" Tomasz asked, somewhat disappointed. "You thought you could court a girl without asking her father? That's disrespectful. Furthermore, it's ignoring God's order of things. The father has the authority, so don't you try weaseling your way around that."

"No, sir, that's not it," Aleksander defended. "I was going to ask her if I could ask her father."

Tomasz was confused. "…She needs to give her permission for you to ask her father?"

"Well, I thought—I felt that…since she doesn't know that I want to court her, I should make her aware first." Aleksander fumbled through his words. "In a way, I'd—I'd be telling her so that I would find out if…she wants to. If she doesn't like me, there would be no need to ask her father."

Tomasz stared at his son for some time. "She doesn't know you like her?"

Aleksander shook his head.

"She doesn't know?" Tomasz asked again.

"No, sir," Aleksander told his father.

"You've invited her over for a couple of months, and she has no idea?"

"No, sir."

"Her father knows," Tomasz pointed out.

"Yes, sir."

"Her brother knows."

"Yes, sir."

"But she doesn't know?" Tomasz repeated.

"No, sir."

Tomasz stood there with amazement and disbelief on his face. He pulled another cigarette from his pocket and instantly began lighting it.

"I'm sorry, sir." Aleksander felt the need to apologize after Tomasz stood there in silence for a few minutes.

Tomasz shook his head. "Don't apologize." The man thought some more before answering his son. "Well, boy, if she doesn't know, go let her know. If she likes you back, you go to her father immediately after, you understand?"

"Yes, sir."

Six roses. Aleksander was told that six roses meant "I want to be yours." He felt that it had the right message and that Liliana would probably know what it meant.

Aleksander had gone over his plan several times in his mind as he arrived at school very early that day. Each time he went over his plan, he became unsure if it was the best way to go about it. What he had originally thought to do was give the roses to Liliana during lunch at school. After he had given her the roses, he would ask her if she was interested in a romantic relationship with him. Assuming she said yes, Aleksander would speak to her father directly after school. Aleksander thought it was bold and daring, and, after having spent all the time with her the past couple of months, he felt that he had a decent chance. After all, it would be a very public display of his desire to court her.

…And that was precisely why he immediately rethought his methods. It would be a very public display of his desire to court her. All of his peers would see it take place, and they would possibly see Liliana very quickly reject him. The mocking and insults would only increase exponentially after that. It would embarrass both him and Liliana.

While sitting at his desk, he began racking his brain for an alternative way. He could wait until after school, go to Liliana's house, and ask her there. But that had its own share of problems, as well. Aleksander had not considered that he had already disrespected Liliana's father by not going to him first. Asking Liliana with her father present might make things worse. Aleksander then considered going to the house and asking to speak with Liliana's father first and then speaking to Liliana, but he still had the roses with him. It would make him seem like he had already assumed Liliana's father's answer.

Aleksander shook his head, frustratedly. No, going to the house after school didn't feel right. Not to mention, he had no guarantee that the flowers would do well for that long. For the moment, they were hidden behind the school.

Aleksander knew that every minute they sat there risked them being found by a person or animal, wilting, or some other unfortunate happenstance.

Giving her the flowers at lunch was more than enough risk. Leaving them there until after school could mean them being lost altogether.

Aleksander then wondered if he could give her the roses at lunch but not say anything. Then, he could speak to her about it when she and Albin came by the farm later. No, that wouldn't work, either. It would seem very odd, and Liliana could've become very confused if no explanation had been given.

"I should have waited to get the flowers after school and then asked her at the farm," Aleksander grumbled inwardly as the rest of the other students began showing up at the schoolhouse.

But it was too late to pull that now. He had the roses here and didn't want to risk them withering any more than they already had today.

Lunch came all too soon. Aleksander's heart was pounding unusually hard. This was it. It was time to ask her the question. As the other students immediately began heading outside, Aleksander took a moment to pray to the Lord above.

After all, God had not given him any obvious no. Aleksander's father even told him that he had given his blessing thus far.

Aleksander had a chance, didn't he?

After all of his other classmates were eating their lunches, Aleksander made his way to the back of the school. He retrieved the roses and slowly made his way to the front of the school.

There was no backing out now.

Thoughts came to Aleksander's mind so

feverishly that he couldn't even truly discern all of them. As he came around the corner, his eyes spotted Liliana immediately. She was around her friends, as usual, but seemed to be looking around for someone.

"Is she looking for me?" Aleksander wondered as his heart kept beating ferociously. *"Is she wondering where I am?"* A few students started seeing Aleksander and his bundle of roses, but Aleksander forced himself to ignore them. He had a mission.

With each step, he felt his nerves become more and more unsettled. But he couldn't stop now! He had to see this through! Even if it meant rejection! He was going to be bold and brave! His actions that day would cement the fact that even if Aleksander Kurtz was to be rejected by the most beautiful girl in Poland, he was no coward!

Still, he was nervous and distracted by the myriad of thoughts that kept shooting through his mind.

And he was so nervous and distracted by his thoughts that he never saw the fist coming.

Piercing hot pain branched into Aleksander's face as knuckles plowed right into his nose. It was a punch coming from Aleksander's left and had enough force behind it to knock the poor boy into the dirt.

Aleksander was disoriented as he tried to slowly pick himself up. Blood began dripping from his nose, and his left eye was already swelling up. He started looking around, trying to make sense of what had just happened.

Then, he saw his bundle of roses. Right in front of

him. A shoe stomped on them, crushing them into the ground. For good measure, the shoe smeared them back and forth into the dirt, completely ruining all six of his roses.

"What did I tell you about ogling my girl, Kurtz?!" Piotr spat.

Aleksander turned his face upward to see that the shoe indeed belonged to Piotr. The tall, young man seemed to be both smiling and sneering at the same time. Aleksander got off the ground and stood to his feet. As he did, three other boys surrounded him. Piotr's friends and fellow bullies. Ones who belittled and mocked Aleksander on a regular basis.

It was clear that they were intending to send a message. The rest of the school area became deathly quiet.

Everyone was watching, including Liliana, but no one dared intervene.

Aleksander pressed his hand to his nose to try and keep the constant blood flow suppressed. He was forced to breathe from his mouth as he eyed each boy who stood around him.

"Apologize," Aleksander demanded darkly.

"Ha!" Piotr bellowed. "You're certainly not in a position to demand anything! You're completely out—" Aleksander had given him a chance. Only one chance.

When it was clear that Piotr was not going to take that chance, Aleksander slugged Piotr in the face. Directly in the nose, just as Piotr had done to him.

The boy screamed as he fell in the dirt, rolling

around in pain.

With that, the three other boys charged at Aleksander.

The first one was easy. Aleksander quickly sidestepped one of the boy's punches, and he accidentally struck his fellow. Aleksander followed with a blow to the first boy's kidney and then an elbow strike to his back. When he simultaneously realized that he had hit his friend and that he himself had been hit, he made a rather strange sound. It was a combination of a gasping-type "Ohh!" someone makes when they understand that they made a mistake, and an "Aah!" sound someone makes when they get hit in the back.

Aleksander then kicked his attacker in the back of the leg, forcing him to the ground. The second boy, who had been hit by the first, was still recovering from the gut punch he had received. The third bully was the sole opponent for the moment. He tried kicking Aleksander, but Aleksander rushed forward at him, so the power of his kick was lost. He still hit Aleksander in the side, but it was with his upper shin.

All Aleksander felt from it was an exaggerated tap. Taking the opportunity of the moment, Aleksander seized the third bully's leg as it made contact with his side. He hobbled momentarily, trying to pull his leg back, but it was no use. Aleksander had hold of it. He then jabbed the boy's leg right in the sensitive thigh. The boy gave a cry right before Aleksander thrust his leg upward, causing him to crash on his back.

Aleksander spun around right as the first two were both coming back at him. Aleksander took the offensive this time. He punched second in the gut, precisely where he had already been hit. This caused him to double over in pain. Aleksander was tempted to add another punch to the jaw since his face was very much in range, but the first boy was throwing another strike. Aleksander dodged it just like before, throwing a carefully aimed stomp to the bully's foot as Aleksander ducked. A couple of sharp pops could be heard as the boy winced. Aleksander then grabbed both boys' heads and slammed them together. They both crumbled to the ground.

Aleksander whipped back around to the third boy, who was standing back up and moving to grab Aleksander.

Aleksander seized his open hands and twisted his fingers violently. He made a sort of "Ah! Ah! Ah! Ah! Ah!" yelp before Aleksander swept at his legs, tripping him. He fell back on his back, and for good measure, Aleksander did an elbow drop on him.

That was enough for the third boy. He simply groaned as he writhed some on the ground.

Aleksander turned back to the other two. They weren't in any hurry to get up either.

The rest of the school kids simply looked at Aleksander in awe, coupled with a fair amount of fear.

After all, the total time of the fight was under a minute. Aleksander wiped more of the blood from his nose again as he spotted Piotr quickly fleeing from him.

Narrowing his eyes in concentrated anger, Aleksander removed one of his shoes. He took a moment to aim and then flung the shoe forcefully. His aim was true, and Piotr was bashed on the back of the head by the shoe. The strike threw him off balance, and he faltered directly next to a tree. A solid tree branch smacked him in the face. Piotr fell back, utterly unconscious.

Now that the bullies were put in their place, all of Aleksander's anger immediately deflated into horrible embarrassment. Not at the way he had defended himself, but the fact that he was standing there, blood all over his face and uniform, only wearing one shoe, a swollen eye that would likely become black, with ripped-up roses.

And everyone was staring at him. This was a much worse scenario than he had ever anticipated.

With what dignity he had left, he picked up his destroyed roses and slowly approached Liliana. Liliana was standing with her friends, her mouth hanging slightly open. The embarrassment compounded with each step he took closer to her, and Aleksander did his best to keep from crying. He couldn't do that now.

When he finally reached Liliana, he cleared his throat. "These flowers—" Aleksander gestured to the pitiful roses as he tried to keep his voice steady. "They were for you. I was going to ask you, Miss Liliana Hodor, if you would be interested in courting me. If you are, I was going to ask your father for his permission to do so. If not, that's perfectly fine. But these flowers are not fit to give to you. So, I am going to buy some new flowers for you and ask you properly."

With that, Aleksander turned away and began heading home. He knew his father wouldn't reprimand him for missing school after everything that happened, and with his uniform stained with blood. On top of it all, Aleksander found himself starting to tear up, and he knew he couldn't bear dealing with the rest of the day if everyone watched him cry in class.

Thankfully, everyone was at his back now, so they couldn't see the tears. Aleksander tried to hold his head high as he strode over to the unconscious Piotr, recovered his shoe, and continued the rest of the way home.

Liliana was completely and utterly dumbfounded. So much had just happened in such a short amount of time. The roses, the fight, the confession…she had no idea what to say or think.

But she didn't have to say anything because all of her friends spoke for her.

"He *does* have eyes for you!" One exclaimed. "Is that a good thing or a bad thing?"

"A very good thing!" Another girl answered. "Did you see how he took out those boys? What a man!"

"The battle of jealousy is won." A girl nodded.

"And he was so gentlemanly with that declaration of love!" One said sweetly.

"Gentlemanly?" Another grimaced. "He acted like

an ape with those boys!"

"They started it; he finished it," The girl returned with a wink.

"It's true; he's never acted out like that before," one pointed out, "and they've been treating him horribly for as long as I can remember. They had it coming."

"Stop," Liliana hushed them all. "Just stop. I need to think this over."

Suddenly, Mr. Laris walked outside the school.

"All right, everyone, time for class again," He proclaimed to all of them. Then he noticed the three boys still lying on the ground. "What happened here?"

Liliana and her friends all glanced at each other before all answering at once.

"They tripped."

"Accidentally headbutted each other."

"Charades."

"They wanted to nap."

"Gas."

Mr. Laris stared at them for a few moments before shrugging. "Whatever, time for class."

CHAPTER SEVEN:
The Answer

Aleksander stared at his house from several meters away. Sitting on the dirt road, he couldn't bring himself to actually walk inside the house and face his father. Aleksander knew Tomasz would never be harsh with him over what had transpired. Tomasz encouraged him to stand up for himself, and if need be, to fight bullies. If anything, he would praise his son for what he did and console him for how the conversation with Liliana did not go as planned.

Aleksander simply didn't want to tell his father that he failed. To be perfectly candid, he had not failed in any form. Piotr had been a brute, and Aleksander dealt with him accordingly. But he felt like a failure, nonetheless, and valued his father's opinion so highly…he couldn't bear to report his "failure" to him.

"Aleksander!" A voice suddenly caught Aleksander's attention.

He turned to see none other than Liliana Hodor running towards him. She was carrying a book in her hand as well as a few rags.

He was stunned to see her running towards him. Liliana Hodor skipped school for little old Aleksander.

Liliana slowed her pace as she drew near to him.

Without a word, she quickly examined Aleksander's face and then began rapidly flipping through pages of the book she had brought. Aleksander inspected the cover; it was a medical book.

"Nosebleeds." Liliana pointed to a certain section, finally finding it. "Let's see…It says they're usually not a medical issue, but that was a nasty punch Piotr gave you."

"Liliana…" Aleksander spoke quietly. "You didn't have to come all this way—"

Liliana tutted at him and pointed for him to sit down. Aleksander obeyed. Liliana sat down next to him, looking back and forth between Aleksander and her book.

"It says here that you need to sit up but lean forward," Liliana instructed. "This will keep the blood from going down your throat."

Aleksander sat more forward, allowing the blood to drip out on the road.

"Now, gently blow your nose," Liliana advised. *"Gently."* Aleksander did so. More blood came out, along with some blood clots.

"Good," Liliana praised as she read through her book one more time. "Now, pinch your nostrils shut with your thumb and finger. Breathe through your mouth as you do this. Hold that for about ten to fifteen minutes. It should help stop the blood flow."

Aleksander nodded as he followed her instructions.

"I also read that this might help." Liliana held out the rags to Aleksander. They were cool and wet. "I

72

read that it will help your nose." She told him. "Put the first one on the bridge of your nose and hold it there for a bit."

Aleksander did so. Since he was now out of arms, Liliana took the other wet rag and gingerly placed it over Aleksander's left eye.

"It will also help the swelling in your eye." She whispered as she held it there. Both young people sat there for around ten minutes, not saying a word. Yet, both felt that the air about them was charged. Aleksander was burning to ask her why she had come after his plan had gone so horribly. Liliana still felt incredibly overwhelmed with all she had seen and heard that day.

But both said nothing.

Eventually, Aleksander took his hand away from his nose to find that the bleeding had stopped. The swelling in his eye had gone down, but he was likely to get a black eye all the same.

The two stood up as Aleksander used the wet cloth on his nose to clean the blood from his face. He could feel that they were about to part ways. Liliana to her home, and Aleksander to his.

He didn't want it to end this way. "I'm sorry," he blurted.

"Sorry?" Liliana looked confused. "What are you sorry about? Piotr was the one who started it."

Aleksander lowered his eyes. "I suppose I'm sorry you saw me like that. Are you afraid of me?"

Liliana smiled gently at Aleksander. "Afraid of you? I was once, but that was before I knew you.

Aleksander, you don't need to apologize for defending yourself. Honestly, I should be saying sorry to you."

Aleksander lifted his gaze to look Liliana in the eye. Liliana shifted uneasily. "I know that they made fun of you for such a long time, but I never did anything about it because I didn't know you, and I thought you were weird. But, really, you're a much more decent fellow than all of them combined. I'm sorry that I never saw that until recently, and I'm sorry I misjudged you. Truly, you're a better person than even I am."

"Don't say that," Aleksander replied softly.

"No, it's true!" Liliana persisted. "I've been conceited and thinking myself better than most people. I thought that I didn't even need the Lord in my life, but you showed me how wrong I was. You've humbled me and made me understand that I am nothing and deserve nothing. Yet, God has blessed me with so much."

Liliana suddenly smiled brightly and confidently. "So, yes."

Aleksander blinked at her. "Yes? Yes, what?"

"Yes, Aleksander." Liliana beamed. "My answer is yes. I would be honored for you to talk to my father about us courting."

With a black eye and a still-recovering nose, Aleksander sat anxiously in the parlor room of the Hodor household. It had been five days since Liliana, and he had agreed to become a couple. That was completely dependent upon what Liliana's father decided, who could not meet with Aleksander until the sabbath due to his busy work schedule. Aleksander was grateful, for he wanted some time to get his thoughts together. He also had hoped that his black eye would dissipate, though he was disappointed in that.

Now, the day had arrived. Aleksander had previously thought he had been scared in the moments before he would ask Liliana. That was nothing compared to the anxiety he felt now. He was about to speak to not only Liliana's father but also a very wealthy businessman.

Approaching the house, Aleksander was blown away by its size and how well-structured it was. Where it wasn't finely cut stone, it was polished, sturdy wood. The inside of the house was immaculate. Even the parlor room he now sat in was lovely. Decorated with pieces of art and very expensive furniture.

However, the beauty of the house only made Aleksander worry. He had nothing to offer in terms of finances. Aleksander ashamedly glanced down at his clothes; they were nice, but rather plain and worn. Appearance-wise, he knew that he was not impressive. Mentally speaking, he was average in his studies. His knowledge of farmwork and animals was not unique. Better candidates could be found in that area other than himself.

Yes, Aleksander felt that he had very little to

offer. Still, God had led Aleksander this far. If it was to face denial from Liliana's father, he purposed to face it with dignity and acceptance. Clearly, if that was the path that the Lord had designed for him, it was so that he would learn something from it.

Albin suddenly came into the parlor. "Mama and Papa will see you now, Aleksander."

Aleksander drew in a breath and clenched his fists with determination, almost looking like he was preparing himself for a fight. He stood up, making sure he stood as straight as possible. He put his shoulders back and walked very deliberately.

He was ready for the worst-case scenario.

Instead, he was blown away by how short the conversation was. Upon meeting Mr. and Mrs. Hodor, he made his intentions clear. Then, with both parents smiling, Jozef Hodor simply said, "What took you so long, son?"

CHAPTER EIGHT:
The Date

Aleksander's state of surprise and euphoria could not be overstated. Though Aleksander didn't show his emotions as well as most, all of the Hodors could easily tell that he was delighted in that moment. Aleksander couldn't believe he had actually gotten Liliana Hodor as his girlfriend.

Now, all he had to do was, as Albin said, "not mess it up."

"So, when are we going to go on a date?" Liliana asked Aleksander a few days later while on their lunch break at school. The two had begun sitting together very regularly at the fixed bench during lunch. They had become quite the schoolhouse gossip, both good and bad. Most of the bad gossip originated from Piotr, and nearly everyone knew it.

Aleksander and Liliana ignored such gossip. Humorously enough, both were already rather used to being the subjects of gossip, so they knew not to let it bother them.

They were, indeed, a couple. That was all anyone needed to know, and they didn't care what anyone else thought of it. Liliana, however, found herself slightly underwhelmed.

She knew this was because she had been in relationships with boys who constantly did everything they could to impress her. They were like fireworks. Exciting, but fleeting. Aleksander, on the other hand, had already demonstrated how he was the opposite. He could have been likened more to a mountain. Not nearly as thrilling as fireworks, but ever-present and unchanging.

Liliana liked that about him. She knew that she wanted someone who would consistently show his true self rather than put on a show until he felt that he had won her. All the same, Liliana was **bored**.

Aleksander said they were forbidden from any physical affection. Liliana knew kissing was off the table, and certainly everything beyond that, but hugging? Leaning on each other? Not even hand-holding?

No, all of those were forbidden by Aleksander himself, which Liliana felt was odd. Usually, a boy would blame his parents for not being able to do anything of the sort. With Aleksander, he said that he forbade them. He said any physical affection was to be saved for marriage.

"Too early to be thinking about that," Liliana thought to herself. *"He isn't really thinking about that already, is he? No, he's probably just being dramatic."*

So, physical affection was out of the question. Liliana could live with that. After all, Aleksander had shown himself to be the kind of person that impressed her more than most, albeit in unorthodox ways. And they had only been officially dating for less than a week. Perhaps a real date would show more of Aleksander's quality.

"A date?" Aleksander considered. "That is something that's done, isn't it?"

"Usually."

"Sorry," Aleksander apologized, "I'm new at this."

"Have you never dated anyone ever before?"

"You're the first," Aleksander confirmed, "and hopefully, the last."

"What?" Liliana blinked at him.

"What?" Aleksander asked back.

The two stared at each other for a few moments. At that moment, they both realized something. For Liliana, she realized that Aleksander was already thinking about marrying her after only being officially a couple for a few days. For Aleksander, he realized that Liliana was **not** thinking about marriage.

"Must be a thing for someone who dates as much as she has," Aleksander concluded inwardly. *"I'm still in her trial period."*

All the same, Aleksander smiled as an idea came to him. "You like *pączki*?" he asked Liliana.

"*Pączki*?" Liliana looked slightly concerned. "Do you know how unhealthy they are?"

"You didn't answer my question."

Liliana paused. "...I **adore** *pączki*. I can't get enough of them."

"I know this place in Danzig that makes the best *pączki* you've ever tasted." Aleksander smiled. "If it's all right with your family, Albin can go with us."

"Danzig?" Liliana raised her eyebrows. "That's

around twenty-four kilometers away from Zaginiony. We can't walk there. I suppose my father could drive us there, but—" But Liliana stopped after seeing Aleksander's wide smile. "What?" She asked.

"What do you think about riding there?" Aleksander asked.

Liliana's eyes doubled in size.

"And this time, I think you're ready to use Kasper at full gallop." Aleksander winked.

"Oh, my soul…" Liliana gasped. "Yes!"

The idea of the trip was brought before both Jozef and Tomasz. Jozef found Albin to be a suitable chaperone, and Tomasz had no objections to letting them borrow three horses for the day.

"In fact, some could really use the exercise," Tomasz observed, "and it might be exciting for them to get out and about. Good idea."

With that, plans were made. Naturally, it couldn't be on a school day, nor could it be on a Sunday due to church.

That left Saturday. Normally, Tomasz wouldn't allow it since he still liked to practice the ceremony of the sabbath with his son. But this was a special instance, and Aleksander was taking this trip not for work but for a date.

"Mind the horses," Tomasz told Aleksander as the three were mounting up on their horses. "Just because you have a pretty girl with you doesn't mean you can ignore them." Aleksander blushed, glancing over at Liliana, who tried to suppress a smile. Albin, however, groaned.

"Make sure you respect Feliks as well," Tomasz ordered. "He tells you to do anything, you do it. Outside of disobeying the Lord."

"Surely Feliks wouldn't ask me to do anything like that," Aleksander countered as he mounted up on his own horse.

"Eh, he's getting up in years." Tomasz shrugged. "Also, be back before too late. Don't make her parents worry about her or her brother."

"He talks about us like we're not here," Liliana whispered to Albin.

"I think it's because he doesn't remember our names," Albin whispered back.

"I will, sir," Aleksander replied to his father.

"And son?"

"Yes, Father?"

Tomasz allowed a warm smile to break through. "Have a great time."

Aleksander smiled back. "Yes, sir."

Liliana finally experienced the kind of riding she really wanted. Now with a bit more experience under her belt, she eased Kasper into his gallop by gradually urging him to go faster. With the wind in her hair and the feeling of freeing exhilaration all about her, Liliana knew she had been born to be around horses. She had known it since she was five years old.

She glanced to her right to see Aleksander easily keeping pace with her.

Aleksander was grinning mischievously, which was very uncharacteristic of him. Then, before Liliana could wonder as to why he was grinning, Aleksander urged his horse onward and sped in front of Liliana.

"Oh, you want a race, do you?" Liliana shouted with glee. "Let's go, Kasper!"

"Wait! No!" Albin shouted to them from behind. "I don't like riding that fast! Wait for me!"

Liliana and Aleksander zoomed ahead of him, completely ignoring his pleas.

"I'm the chaperone!" Albin screeched at them, his voice cracking. "Don't abandon the chaperone! Father will have your hide!"

With that, he reluctantly urged his own horse faster. Meanwhile, Aleksander and Liliana were neck and neck, racing towards an unknown finish line. Both were laughing as first place was constantly shifting between them. Liliana knew that Aleksander was going easy on her. There was no other explanation. He had grown up around horses and was an expert rider. And Liliana was determined to make him regret underestimating her. She urged Kasper on even more, inching ahead of Aleksander and then pulling out in front of him. She constantly checked behind her, making sure Aleksander had no opportunity to get around her.

"Keep your eyes ahead of you!" Aleksander called out to her.

"You only say that because you want to pass me!" Liliana shot back.

"Always a competition with you!" Aleksander responded. "Maybe I just want you safe! Have you considered that?" Liliana shook her head, still smiling. It seemed like everyone wanted her safe. And she knew why. The world was dangerous, and she was often reckless. Whenever someone asked her to do something for her own safety, she often kicked against it, claiming that she could take care of herself.

But Liliana didn't do that this time. She turned her eyes strictly forward, heeding Aleksander's words. She began to reflect on this while she gently started pulling on Kasper's reins, beginning to slow him down.

Why was she so willing to listen to Aleksander when she used to be rather stubborn with others, including her own father? She found that there were several reasons actually. Getting injured or unintentionally harming Kasper again were rather high on that list, but she also found that she was open to accepting influence from Aleksander. He had shown himself to be humble, so he wasn't asking her to be careful because he thought himself better skilled than her (even though he was). Nor was he doing it because he thought Liliana incapable, as many other people had. If he thought Liliana incapable, he would not have suggested riding in the first place, and he certainly wouldn't have raced against her. Liliana felt like Aleksander saw her as an equal, which wasn't too terribly common for her when it came to boys. Thus, there was only one

83

reason that Aleksander asked her to be careful: it was because he was concerned for her. That was all. Not some game of injured pride or a need for control. Just basic, human decency.

Liliana slowed Kasper down to a walk as Kasper was taking deep breaths. Aleksander had slowed down his horse as well, walking right up beside Liliana. The two said nothing but simply smiled at each other.

"You rascals!" They suddenly heard far behind them. Both turned about to see Albin, still a good way off. He was riding as fast as he was able, looking frightfully irritated.

"We seem to be in trouble," Aleksander chuckled.

"Once he gets some *pączki*, all will be forgiven," Liliana smirked.

Before riding into the city of Danzig, Aleksander told Liliana and Albin that they would have to drop their horses off at a friend's. He lived a few kilometers outside of Danzig on a farm of his own. He was waiting for them when they came down his road.

"Aleksander!" The elderly man waved to the riders as they approached. "Shalom, shalom!"

"Shalom, shalom, Feliks!" Aleksander answered back. Albin and Liliana glanced at each other.

"Shalom?" Albin mouthed to his sister. Liliana simply shrugged in response.

As they drew up to the house, Liliana took a good look at Feliks. Once she did, she tried not to stare. The man looked oddly cartoonish. He had a nose that looked too big for his face. He was balding on the top of his head but had a ring of grey hair that, strangely enough, seemed to poof out. Aside from that, the man just looked overly happy. ***Too*** happy. Like he was actively trying to be jovial.

"Hey, how's that young boy treating you out there?" Feliks nudged Aleksander after he had dismounted.

"Father treats me very well, sir," Aleksander answered as the two embraced.

Feliks then turned to Liliana. "Ah, this must be the beautiful young lady I've heard so much about."

"Not you too…" Albin whined.

Liliana, on the other hand, giggled, accepting the praise. She turned to Aleksander. "Aw, did you tell him about me?" Aleksander said nothing but began turning a soft red.

"That speaks volumes," Feliks laughed heartily. "Well, now, this old man shan't take any more of your precious time. Aleksander, take this one into the barn. I've some oats waiting for each of them. As for you two, hand over those beauties, will you?"

Aleksander began walking his horse around the house towards the barn. Liliana walked Kasper a bit closer before dismounting and passing Kasper over to Feliks. Feliks took the reins, patting the beast gently as he whispered soothingly to it. He held out his other hand for the reins to Albin's horse, who brought his over promptly. Before long, the three horses were enjoying a few well-earned snacks in the stables.

"Is there anything else you need, sir?" Aleksander asked Feliks.

Feliks suddenly donned a more serious face as he nodded. The elderly man dug in his pocket and pulled out a sealed envelope. He held it out to Aleksander.

"Make sure this gets to Tomasz," Feliks spoke quietly. "It's something he really needs to hear about."

"Yes, sir," Aleksander answered as he took the envelope and tucked it away in his own pocket.

"Now, go have fun." Feliks lightened up again, smiling brightly. "Shalom, shalom."

"'Shalom, shalom," Aleksander replied.

"What's 'Shalom, shalom'?" Liliana asked Aleksander as they made their way into the streets of Danzig.

Aleksander was very surprised at this. "You don't know what shalom means?"

"It doesn't sound very Polish," Albin brought up.

"Well, it's not." Aleksander shrugged as he scratched his head. "It's Hebrew."

"Hebrew?" Liliana questioned. "You're Jewish?"

"I am." Aleksander nodded. "Honestly, I have no idea how that never came up before."

"Whoa." Albin marveled. "So, you're the descendants of the people in the Bible?"

Aleksander nodded proudly.

"Which tribe?" Liliana asked, also eager to know.

"Benjamin."

"I was hoping for Judah." Albin sighed with

disappointment.

"Yeah, sorry." Aleksander laughed. "That tribe is everyone's favorite. David, Solomon, Jesus. But, hey, we get Saul and Paul."

"That means you're prophesied to ravin as a wolf," Liliana remembered from Genesis.

Aleksander shrugged. "That's more to the tribe as a whole than individuals."

"So, wait, you believe in Jesus?" Albin interrogated.

"Yes," Aleksander confirmed, slightly unsure of where Albin was going with that.

"You're very Jewish to believe in Jesus." Albin squinted at him.

"So was Peter," Aleksander replied. "And the rest of the Apostles. And Nicodemus. And Jesus Himself. Being Jewish doesn't mean I can't be Christian."

"Fair point." Albin conceded.

"You don't have anything against Jews, do you?" Aleksander asked both of them.

Liliana and Albin glanced at each other.

"We've heard nasty things about Jews," Liliana confessed.

"From who?"

"Mostly the news," Albin pointed out. "Our father likes to listen to the radio late at night, and we can sometimes hear it."

Aleksander was unsettled by this. What radio would be broadcasting ideas that the Jewish people are relatively unpleasant? What had any of them done?

"It's probably all rumors and idle gossip anyway," Liliana dismissed. "We've never known any Jews until now, and look at you! You're amazing! Nothing near what they say."

That got Aleksander smiling again. "Yeah, just idle gossip."

The conversation drifted off as the group entered the fabled *pączki* bakery that Aleksander had told Liliana and Albin about so much.

Aleksander spoke with the merchant and quickly placed an order for eighteen *paczki*.

"Eighteen?" Liliana marveled. "Isn't that a bit excessive?"

"It is a special occasion," Aleksander told her. "Besides, we can take our time. We don't have to eat all of them right now."

"Says who?" Albin shouted excitedly. "I'll take whatever she doesn't eat!"

"Let's just start with six for you and see how you feel after that," Aleksander laughed. "Besides, we're not eating them here."

"We're not?" Liliana asked.

"No." Aleksander smiled. "The best place to eat a *paczki* is in the sky."

The town hall—said to have been built in the 14th century. The first and foremost thing that stuck out about it was the clock tower, which reached up to around eighty-one meters high. That was their destination.

"I've been up here before with my father," Aleksander explained as they climbed the numerous steps up into the tower. "It has the best view. Much taller than anything we have in Zaginiony. Unfortunately, he hasn't been able to climb these steps for quite a while."

"I can understand why!" Albin despaired from the back, wheezing as he slowly climbed the stairs behind Aleksander and Liliana.

But even Albin stopped complaining once they reached the top of the tower. Being a gorgeous summer day with clear skies, they could see out for kilometers. Not only did it overlook the town of Danzig itself, but past the city into the trees and hills beyond.

"This is where you eat *paczki*." Aleksander smiled as he enjoyed the two Hodors' awe. He opened the box, and the three enjoyed the jelly-filled delights as they gazed out over the glorious sights before them.

"Did you know I once ate ice cream while sitting on the edge of the railing up here?" Aleksander asked with a devilish grin.

Albin glanced at the railing. "You sat on that?"

"I did."

"Did you get in trouble?"

"Oh, yes." Aleksander nodded. "They'll kick you out if you try that."

Albin paused, "…But now I feel like I have to do it, too."

"If you want to live to see another day, I'd advise not attempting that," Liliana warned flatly. "We'll get thrown out, I'll tell Father, and there will suddenly be a new grave in our cemetery."

"What if I tell Father you two tried to escape me?" Albin shot back, sticking out his tongue.

"We did nothing of the sort." Liliana narrowed her eyes at him.

"You did so."

"We were racing."

"Semantics," Albin dismissed. "So, I keep your secret, and you keep mine, eh?"

There was a lengthy silence between the three. Aleksander peered over the edge of the tower.

"No one's looking," he whispered to the other two.

Liliana huffed, "Fine. Make it quick."

After Albin's death-defying deed of rebellion (which only lasted ten seconds), the three sat in a prolonged quiet as they enjoyed their *paczki* and looked out over the city from different sides of the tower.

"This is strangely nice," Liliana finally sighed as she finished her third *pączek*. "Most boys want to take me someplace exciting."

"Are you disappointed?" Aleksander asked apprehensively.

"I am, but not in you," Liliana answered. "I think I'm a little disappointed in myself."

"Why?" Aleksander questioned, slightly confused.

"Because I found out that I like thrills," Liliana admitted, staring at the beautiful view. "Most times, at the expense of what is truly good for me."

"How do you mean?" Aleksander queried.

"The first time I rode Kasper." Liliana pulled

from her memory. "I think that summarizes it up perfectly. I sought the thrill, and I definitely got it, but what I did was not only potentially very harmful to me but to Kasper as well. I think I did that with past boyfriends. I sought out something exciting, someone handsome…and I was always so confused as to why my parents constantly disapproved. It was because that boy was harmful to me. And I was to him, too, in the state I was in. I wasn't looking for someone I could share the rest of my life with. I was looking for someone who made me happy."

Liliana glanced down as she felt Aleksander's gaze on her. "Nothing wrong with wanting to be happy, of course, but I think that's **all** I was focused on. I only cared about my own happiness, not anyone else's. I was so self-centered. I still am, probably."

Then, taking a breath, she lifted her eyes and gazed out at the view once more. "This is nice. Not exactly exciting. Going back to the horse analogy, the full gallop on Kasper was great, but I find that the times when we rode slowly as we talked are far dearer to me now. The same with today. We just stood up here, beholding the Lord's beautiful creation, and we talked. I learned more about you, and you about me. That, I think, is the essence of what a relationship should be. Not trying to impress each other over and over again. Just beholding all the great things God has done while we talk together."

"That was beautiful," Aleksander praised.

"I have my moments," Liliana laughed as she turned to Aleksander. "Thank you for taking me up here. I really, *really* enjoyed myself."

"Likewise." Aleksander beamed back.

Meanwhile, Albin, on the other side of Aleksander, rolled his eyes. "Just marry each other already! I do *not* want to keep being exposed to these lovey-dovey conversations forever!"

CHAPTER NINE:
Storm Clouds

Tomasz was pleased to hear that his son's date with Liliana had gone well. But a bad omen returned with the boy: a letter from Feliks.

Tomasz knew that if Old Man Feliks said he needed to hear something, it wasn't good news. Tomasz dreaded opening that letter, but he knew it was important if it came from Feliks.

Feliks was crucial during the war. He had acted as a source of information on the Germans. Feliks was good at traveling and very good at looking completely innocent and harmless. He was also fluent in several different languages and always smarter than he let on. Feliks often played the happy-go-lucky fool to get people to relax around him.

Tomasz's hands trembled slightly as he opened the envelope. Once he spread out the letter on his desk, he found it was all written in gibberish.

"Oh no…" He muttered to himself. It was coded, which meant that it was likely worse than Tomasz originally thought. Tomasz analyzed it for a second before going over to his dresser. Taking out the bottom drawer altogether, Tomasz found an old folder and a half-filled cigarette pack.

He grinned to himself. *"The boy never thinks to look here."*

Taking the folder and a solitary cigarette, Tomasz

made his way back over to his desk to decipher the letter.

Tomasz was about to light the cigarette when he suddenly heard a *"tch"* sound. Tomasz turned in his seat to find his son standing in his room's doorway. Aleksander was eyeing the cigarette in Tomasz's mouth with the utmost contempt, but the boy said nothing.

Tomasz paused, knowing that Aleksander would never outright ask him to throw away his cigarette. Eventually, Aleksander would just walk away.

"Father, I was going to boil some water," Aleksander suddenly spoke, his anger suddenly vanishing.

Tomasz simply blinked at Aleksander, wondering where he was going with this.

"We seem to be out of matches to light the stove. Can I use your lighter?" Aleksander pointed at the lighter on Tomasz's desk.

"Well played," Tomasz thought as he sighed dejectedly. Without saying anything, Tomasz held out the lighter to Aleksander, who quickly snatched it and walked off. "Bring that back when you're done with it," Tomasz called grumpily after his son. "It was a gift from a friend."

Tomasz spat out the cigarette as he returned to Feliks' letter. He opened the old folder he had kept from the war. There were several keys to codes that he had compiled after the Treaty of Versailles. He knew his memory would fail him after so long, and he wanted to still be able to decipher such codes.

After meticulously translating Feliks' letter, Tomasz read it all at once:

> "I've been to Germany lately. Things have changed, and not for the better. This Hitler fellow…he's a plague. An insane man, but a very skilled orator. His speeches are carefully tailored to each audience. Satan's power surrounds him. There is a palpable and growing anger towards our people in Germany. Tomasz, something is coming. I will keep a close eye on this. See to it that you and your boy pray diligently for our people and that the fires of war are not rekindled."

Tomasz walked out of his room and into the kitchen, where Aleksander was cooking dinner. Aleksander noticed the melancholy atmosphere that came with his father.

"Are you all right, Father?" Aleksander asked as Tomasz sauntered into the room.

Tomasz simply held his hand out. Aleksander promptly returned his father's lighter. Tomasz then struck it, sparking a small flame. He put the letter over the flame, lighting it on fire.

"Pray for the peace of Jerusalem, my son," Tomasz said somberly as he discarded the burning letter into the metal wastebasket.

"I do, sir," Aleksander responded, feeling somewhat worried by his father's mood.

Tomasz walked over to the window and gazed out. "See to it you pray for the peace of our people in every land, as well."

"I will," Aleksander told his father. "Is something happening?"

Tomasz gazed at his son. Aleksander was tough, true, but Aleksander had never seen war. Tomasz had no desire to prepare his son for that, either. Besides, Aleksander had been so jubilant as of late, what with getting the girl of his dreams.

Tomasz, right or wrong, didn't want to douse a happy moment with these ominous signs on the horizon. "No." Tomasz smiled at his son. "I'm just making sure you keep our nation and people in your prayers every day. It's important."

"Yes, sir."

One year passed. Things went on as they always had. In that time, Tomasz began to relax, not hearing anything new from Feliks. Meanwhile, Aleksander's life was growing all the brighter. He and Liliana became closer and closer, eventually being totally inseparable. The two went from admiration, to friendship, to love.

Does that mean they were terribly romantic and doting towards one another, calling each other pet names all the time? No, in fact, they were often very quiet around one another, but they enjoyed that. They expressed their fondness towards each other in a rather unique way that some might consider indifference. However, anyone who was watching would see the light in both of their eyes in how they looked at one another. They would feel the ease that the two felt in each other's presence. The contented joy of just being with one another.

They knew they were in love, and so did everyone else who looked close enough.

Had Aleksander been wealthier, he would have asked Liliana to marry him several months ago. Liliana knew this as well and often told Aleksander that her father was willing to help him financially. But the boy was unmoved. He would not ask for any money from anyone, especially Mr. Hodor. He was going to build up his funds through his own work ethic. This kind of determination made both Tomasz and Jozef incredibly proud. Aleksander was less like a boy and more like a man, only looking to the Lord for aid.

Tomasz knew his son would be all right, and Jozef had the same confidence for his daughter.

But unfortunately, things do not always go as planned…

Tomasz felt troubled in his sleep one night around the beginning of October. He dreamt of a man who continually pursued him, laughing manically. Everything the man touched burst into flames. Tomasz was continually running, but the laughing man was just one step behind him. The fire was growing fiercer. The laughing was growing louder. Smoke was choking him. He could barely breathe!

Tomasz awoke with a start when he realized he truly was having difficulty breathing. The dream had forced itself into reality! At least, that was what he originally thought. Instead, he perceived that there was smoke that was filling his room. Not the cigarette smoke that he was used to.

No, this was smoke from a blazing conflagration. Coughing uncontrollably, just trying to breathe, Tomasz struggled to stumble out of his bed. He pulled himself up to his window to find the entire farm…was on fire.

Tomasz couldn't even speak; he was so stunned. Not only that, but he was still coughing without respite. The fumes in the air were enough to smother any person, much less him. As quickly as he was able, he made his way outside. Unbeknownst to both Tomasz and Aleksander during the night, a storm had rolled in. Not uncommon in the autumn time. But a solitary lightning bolt had split a tree on the edge of their farm. It had been relatively dry as of late, and it was just enough to cause a blaze to produce quickly. The fire rapidly spread to the old, worn buildings. Tomasz had remained asleep while Aleksander had heard the shrieking of animals.

"The laughter…" Tomasz understood. The laughter in his dream was actually Tomasz hearing the animals cry out, but as Tomasz thought on this in horror, he spotted his son. Aleksander had just burst through their largest barn, allowing all of the horses to run free—and not a moment too soon, for the barn was more fire than wood now, and it began collapsing. Aleksander moved surprisingly quickly, getting out of reach of the crumbling, smoking structure.

Tomasz grasped his chest, thanking the Lord that

Aleksander had moved out of the way. But Tomasz's worry revived as he witnessed Aleksander race to another one of the ablaze buildings, trying to rescue more animals.

"Son!" Tomasz tried to yell, but his coughing forbade him. He stumbled forward to go to Aleksander, waving one of his arms to try and flag the boy down, but it was no use.

Aleksander didn't see him.

Tomasz didn't give up. His son was infinitely more important than any of the animals. Most of them were destined for slaughter anyway. But not his son! No, not his son!

"Aleksa—" Tomasz wheezed, breaking out into his fits of coughing again. "Aleksander!"

Tomasz's vision was starting to waver as he found breathing more and more difficult. He was feeling too weak. His legs were buckling. He fell onto the dusty ground, just struggling to breathe.

"Aleksander…" He called weakly. "Aleksander, my boy…"

Tomasz awoke in a hospital. There were no hospitals in Zaginiony, so Tomasz immediately discerned he had to be in Danzig. He felt an oxygen mask on his face that was helping him breathe after the overwhelming encounter with the smoke.

He turned to find his son sitting next to his bed. Aleksander had his head down on the bed, completely asleep.

"How long have you been waiting there?" Tomasz wondered, relieved to see his boy all right.

99

The position Aleksander was sleeping in was not a comfortable one, so Tomasz knew that Aleksander was only asleep due to exhaustion. Physical, emotional, or more than likely, both. Tomasz closed his eyes and said a quick prayer of thanks to the Lord. He didn't know the state of their farm, but he and Aleksander were both alive.

That was enough.

"You're awake," A voice called from the doorway. Tomasz slowly turned to the voice that came from the doorway. It was none other than Feliks.

"What happened?" Tomasz asked slowly and quietly. After just that simple sentence, he began coughing once more.

"It's best you don't speak, young man," Feliks told him gently as he walked into the room. "Your poor lungs weren't in the best condition even before the fire. I'll tell you all that little Aleksander has told me."

Feliks pulled a stool over to the other side of the hospital bed. "We're not sure who or what started the fire. In his passion, Aleksander blames one of his schoolmates by the name of Piotr. Says he's made Piotr mad on a number of occasions. Regardless, the farm is lost."

Tomasz let out a shuddering, troubled breath at that. Feliks nodded sadly. "Most of the animals escaped due to Aleksander's bravery. He told me none of the horses perished. Most of the dairy cows and chickens got out, too. But the beef cattle didn't make it."

Feliks then put on an awkward smile. "On the bright side, it will smell like well-done steak around your farm for the foreseeable future."

Tomasz gave a slight glare to Feliks.

"Sorry." Feliks cleared his throat. "I had to try."

Tomasz shook his head mournfully. "All...I had...Farm was...all I had."

"Now, now..." Feliks patted the man on the shoulder. "Remember the Psalms, my friend. 'I have been young, and now am old; yet have I not seen the righteous forsaken, nor his seed begging bread.' And let me tell you, Tomasz, I certainly fall into that category of old. Jehovah Jireh will still take care of you."

But Tomasz was still very troubled. He looked frightened and angry even in the midst of his terrible coughs.

"It's best not to think too much about all this right now." Feliks tried to calm Tomasz down. "You need to focus on resting and getting better. The hopeful news is that your house was completely untouched by the fire."

"Doesn't matter," Tomasz growled before coughing again.

"If you need any help, I'm happy to oblige." Feliks offered. "I have some money, Tomasz, I can help—"

"No," Tomasz growled with bared teeth.

"Let go of that pride, boy," Feliks warned with a glare of his own. "Think not of just yourself, but your son. Take the help that you need."

"I said—" Tomasz had to stop because of his coughing. "I said no. I am a man, and I will take care of myself and my own."

"Stubbornness. Stubbornness," Feliks grunted with a heated breath as he stood back up. "A real man knows when to accept help. Tribe of Benjamin indeed."

"What's that supposed…to mean?" Tomasz scowled.

"Read your Old Testament, sir," Feliks retorted as he began to walk out. "See what Samuel said about stubbornness."

Feliks reached the door and was about to go out into the hallway.

"Wait," Tomasz called weakly. Feliks halted.

"Hitler…" Tomasz rasped. "News?"

Feliks took a deep breath before turning back to see Tomasz. "I returned to Germany recently, yes."

"And?" Tomasz asked, the fear growing in his eyes. Feliks paused for the longest time, thinking over the speeches he heard, the cruelty he witnessed, the satanic ideologies in both young and old Germans…

"I believe…it is as we feared, Tomasz," he spoke quietly. "He's defying the Treaty of Versailles. He's rearming Germany. He's ordered submarines. The Nazi party flag with the swastika is now the national flag of Germany, per his order. Last year, he declared himself Führer. He's not doing all of this for nothing."

Tomasz took all of this in, looking at his son, who had stayed asleep on his hospital bed during their entire conversation.

"Thank you, Feliks," Tomasz murmured.

Feliks softened at that. "Think over my offer, Tomasz. I can help you both. Pray about it, will you?"

Tomasz only nodded, and Feliks exited the room.

CHAPTER TEN:

A Promise Given

"I've made a decision," Tomasz announced as he and his son stood on a hill of their property, beholding the charred remains of their farm.

After Aleksander had freed what animals he could, he spotted his father collapsed in the dirt. Desperate to save him, Aleksander carried Tomasz to their neighbor, the closest person with a car.

Doing so left the fire to completely destroy their entire property. Aleksander's neighbor had told his wife to warn other inhabitants of Zaginiony about the fire, as it could easily spread to the town. As he raced Aleksander and Tomasz to Danzig, his wife warned everyone in town.

Zaginiony had no Fire Guard like Warsaw, especially one far out in the country. Only volunteers to help put out local fires. Since it was so dry of late, as many men as possible were mustered to fight the fires. However, the fire had miraculously been put out before the volunteers even reached the farm. Everything was burned, save Tomasz's house.

Upon Aleksander and Tomasz's return, both took time to give thanks and bow in worship. They both knew it was the mercy of Jesus that the fire had not taken everything. With how big the flames were and how dry the surrounding area was, the fire should have claimed much more than the little patch it did.

Because the house still stood, not only did Aleksander and Tomasz still have all of their belongings, but Tomasz still had his stash of emergency money. Something tucked away just in case something like this occurred.

As he began counting it on his desk, he spotted the letter from Nina that still lay on his desk. As he stared at it, he thought of all that Feliks had told him about Germany. Not too long after, he and Aleksander went outside to view the destruction that had taken place. Every farm building was destroyed beyond repair. The horses had all been saved, along with many other animals, but none of them had come back. Tomasz and Aleksander had been gone for so long that any animal that might have come back probably realized no one was going to feed them here.

…Or they were killed and eaten by a wild animal.

Regardless, the Kurtz Farm was non-existent now. They had no means of their previous livelihood. And Aleksander knew, even without hearing the conversation between Feliks and Tomasz, that his father was not going to ask for a single *złoty* from anyone. They were in this mess, and they were going to get themselves out with only the Lord's help.

Aleksander dwelt on that idea with some concern. His father had often said it, but it seemed rather contradictory. Could not the Lord use other people as a means of His help? All in all, it seemed to be based on Tomasz's pride. Aleksander understood that Tomasz struggled with that vice, or else his father might have listened to him about being done with his smoking.

"I've made a decision," Tomasz repeated to his son, bringing Aleksander out of his deep thoughts.

Tomasz looked uncertain about the statement he was about to say. He looked almost afraid, like saying the next statement was very hard for him to do.

All the same, he said it.

"We're leaving," he told Aleksander.

Aleksander had predicted this. Rebuilding the farm would be long and arduous. Tomasz would not be able to do it in his condition. Aleksander himself could do it, but he needed to finish his education. He wouldn't be able to do both in the amount of time needed. After all, their emergency money would only last so long. Even if the farm was rebuilt, animals would then need to be purchased. All in all, it seemed that it was time for a different way of life.

"To Danzig?" Aleksander asked hopefully. He was too frightened to hope that they would stay in Zaginiony. Danzig, however, wasn't too far, and he would still be able to visit Liliana without much difficulty. Not to mention, they would have all the more excuse to revisit the clock tower where they had their first date.

But Tomasz dashed those hopes.

"No," Tomasz shook his head, not looking his son in the eye. "We're leaving for America."

Aleksander was astounded. The United States of America? It made no sense. A different country altogether? One that had a language that was so vastly different, a culture that was so vastly different. Even if they were to leave for a different country, why America? It was a country that was across the Atlantic. Why not something closer, like Lithuania? Czechoslovakia? Romania? Certainly not Germany or the Soviet Union, but there were much closer options than *America!*

For several moments, Aleksander found himself unable to speak. Unable to find the words. Tomasz knew this, too, as he watched his son in his peripheral vision. He dreaded bringing this upon his son, but he felt it was the best option.

After all, America was doing well. Nina herself had said so. It would be far away from any of the coming conflict with Hitler. They would be safe. Things would be very different, but they would have grand opportunities in America.

And they would be safe.

"But…Liliana…" Aleksander finally found some words. Tomasz glanced at his son with sad eyes. Aleksander, in that moment, looked so hurt and confused. Tomasz knew he was bringing significant harm to his son, and he hated himself for it.

However, Tomasz knew that Aleksander was reasonable and once he provided the information, Aleksander would understand. Tomasz opened his mouth to explain. But then, he stopped. Guilt struck him, for he knew several things about this plan of his.

Firstly, he had not prayed about it. How

hypocritical of him, telling Aleksander to constantly pray about large decisions, yet he himself did not. Tomasz was making this decision without concern for the will of God.

Secondly, he knew that his fears concerning Hitler and Germany were only conjecture. Yes, Germany was preparing for war, but that did not necessarily mean that it would come to that.

Thirdly, there were other options. Going to America was not the only course of action. Tomasz very easily could have taken Feliks' offer and stayed with him. He could have even asked the Hodors, who were basically considered family at this point. They had well enough means to provide for both Tomasz and Aleksander. They would even earn their keep, Tomasz knew, for both men didn't rest easy unless they worked.

No, Tomasz's decision was made out of fear and pride. He knew it, and he knew that Aleksander would realize that as well. Aleksander might come to resent him or even hate him if he explained his reasoning.

He knew the boy loved Liliana Hodor, and he knew that it was his selfishness that was taking Aleksander away from her.

So, instead of telling him the truth, Tomasz simply knelt before his son and said, "You have to trust me that I know what is best for us, son."

Aleksander fought the urge to cry. He fought, but he lost that battle. Tears began welling up in his eyes and started to stream down his face.

"I do trust you, sir," Aleksander whimpered quietly. "Whatever you decide, I will follow."

Albin Hodor answered the door to find a red-eyed Aleksander.

"Oh no…" he swallowed. "What's happened?"

"Albin, if you would be so kind as to fetch Liliana for me," Aleksander murmured hoarsely. "I would like to speak with her alone. But don't worry, we'll just be out here where everyone can still see us from the windows. But I would like to talk with just Liliana, please."

Albin nodded and immediately ran off.

When Liliana was alerted, she was relieved she would finally get to speak to Aleksander. She had not seen him since before the fire. She wanted to know if he was all right. She had heard how Aleksander himself had gone into burning buildings to save the animals, and he could have easily gotten hurt. However, she tried not to worry herself too much, for she knew that Aleksander had been to the hospital of Danzig and had returned. Surely the doctors would have treated any ailment that Aleksander had been dealt. Furthermore, she wanted to discuss what was to happen next. She, like Aleksander, knew that Kurtz Farm was finished and that Tomasz would likely not ask for any money from anyone. Knowing this, Liliana had gone over all the possible outcomes and made various preparations concerning them.

Liliana exited her front door to find Aleksander

gazing at the dirt with the most melancholy expression she had ever seen.

"Not good..." Liliana thought to herself.

She quietly approached Aleksander as she analyzed him. He seemed fine, physically speaking. She noticed no bruises, burns, or other injuries. His breathing was normal, which meant the smoke likely had not done any long-term damage. But she could easily tell that he was anything but fine when it came to his emotions. He avoided eye contact with her and fiddled with his hands. Above all, he looked so terribly sad.

"Are you okay?" Liliana asked him. "How's your father?"

"Fine. We're both fine," Aleksander mumbled. "Father was having some trouble breathing, so he was admitted to the hospital. But now, all things considered, he's relatively well."

"And?" Liliana pressed, curious to know the dreadful news that Aleksander was obviously here for. She wasn't eager for it, by any means, but she had several arguments already prepared for them and was more than ready to try and persuade Aleksander and even Tomasz from going through with it.

Aleksander, however, almost felt that he could not bring himself to tell her, so he stayed silent for the longest time. "Aleksander, please talk to me," Liliana said gently. "What's happened?"

Aleksander took a deep breath. "We're leaving."

"Leaving where?"

"To..." Aleksander closed his eyes. "To

110

America."

Liliana was taken aback by this. She had expected Tomasz and Aleksander to move, but not so remarkably far. This was, without a doubt, a death sentence to Aleksander and Liliana's relationship. Moving continents away basically guaranteed them never even seeing each other again, let alone being able to keep a romance thriving. Liliana rapidly thought as to why Tomasz would want to move all the way to America. It made little sense.

Unless…

"Your father's trying to separate you and me," Liliana accused.

"No, he's not." Aleksander dismissed.

"Then why else?" Liliana questioned, her voice revealing her agitation. "Why else move to the other side of the world? It makes no sense."

"We have a relative in America," Aleksander excused.

"One that you're *very* close with, I imagine?" Liliana remarked sarcastically.

Aleksander pursed his lips. "Well…no."

"Exactly." Liliana nodded, growing a bit more angry. "Does your father not approve of me anymore? Think I'm stealing away his son?"

"I told you, Liliana, that's not it," Aleksander told her. "My father is not one to give his blessing lightly, and he did so. Even if he had objections now, he would say them. He speaks his mind. If he disapproved, he would have said so and not manipulated things by moving to force us to split up."

"Then what are his reasons?" Liliana interrogated.

Aleksander hesitated. "...He simply asked me to trust him, and I do."

Liliana grunted angrily. "Of course he did! That's the answer of someone who doesn't have a good reason."

"Liliana, I didn't come to fight about my father..." Aleksander argued.

"No, you came to end our relationship, didn't you?" Liliana started pivoting her anger from Tomasz to Aleksander.

"No, I—"

"It doesn't have to be that way." Liliana tried to cool herself down. She knew this might happen, and so she remembered the convincing arguments she had conceived. "Whatever your father's reasoning, we can convince him together to stay. I've already spoken with my father, and he's agreed to house the both of you here."

"Here?"

"We have wealth, Aleksander." Liliana gestured to her home. She even smiled, sufficiently calming herself. "More than enough to take care of you and your father. And I know that you two both don't like accepting gifts of money, so it will only be until you two can get enough funds to take care of yourselves."

"You and I can't live in the same household, Liliana." Aleksander waved his hands. "There would be too much temptation."

"Then marry me," Liliana offered with a bright

smile.

Aleksander's face began to flush. Of course, the two had spoken about it. They both knew they loved one another and both desired marriage, but no proposal had been given. Until now, technically.

Liliana began blushing as well, noticing Aleksander's face. She messed with her hair some, as she felt an ember of anxiety grow within her.

Aleksander wasn't answering. Had she misjudged everything, and he didn't actually want to marry her?

"Say something," Liliana whispered after waiting so long.

"I…I would." Aleksander fumbled out.

Liliana frowned, her ember of anxiety turning into a roaring flame of horror.

"Would?" She asked, somewhat breathless.

"Yes, I would, but—" Aleksander started to say.

"But?" Liliana cut him off. "But *what?* I just gave you the answer to your problems, Aleksander. Together, we'll talk to your father and persuade him to stay here. Right? Right?"

But Aleksander was already shaking his head. "My father would never allow it. I know him. He's steadfast in his decision. He is determined to move to America."

Liliana felt an explosion of fear and anger mixing together inside her. *"He's choosing his father over me…"*

"Then let him go," Liliana suddenly burst. "If he wants to become a Yankee, let him leave. But you, you stay here. You stay with me. After all, a man leaves his father and his mother and cleaves to his wife, right?"

Aleksander shook his head again, slowly and sadly. "I can't. You know, as well as I, that if I abandon my father, he will die. He can't do hard work in his condition. Forsaking him to work alone in America, where nothing but labor awaits him, would be a death sentence." Aleksander closed his eyes as he felt the urge to cry coming again. "And though you are right: a man is to leave his father and his mother and cling to his wife…we have to acknowledge that you and I are not married. Since we are not married, my duty to my father comes first, as stated by the fifth commandment."

Liliana was breathing faster, tears coming to her own eyes. But where Aleksander was sorrowful, Liliana was angry. "So, I'm not enough for you?" Liliana asked as the tears began falling. "Your father's more important to you than me? Is that it? Because, Aleksander, let me tell you that my parents do not come in my heart before you."

"They should," Aleksander told her. "You are to honor them more than you honor me. I am not your husband."

"But I want you to be!" Liliana shouted at him. "I love you, you imbecile! I want to marry you! Have children with you! Eat *pączki* with you! Grow old with you! But you're deserting me!"

"This is not my choice." Aleksander tried to calm her. He placed his hands on her shoulders, but she pulled herself away.

114

"Don't you dare!" She snarled. "Don't you touch me! It *is* your choice! You're a man, Aleksander! Not some dependent, witless child! You have the ability to stay with me, but you choose against it because...because...!" Liliana shouted in frustration. "I don't even know why! Other than the fact that you don't love me in return! Is that it? You'd rather have some American girl rather than me?! You liked Liliana Hodor as a pretty face, but then you found you couldn't stand how I am?! Is that it, Aleksander?!"

Aleksander suddenly took his shirt and ripped it in twain, exposing his bare chest.

Liliana's mouth was immediately stopped. She blinked, suddenly afraid, strangely impressed, and altogether confused all at the same time. Aleksander had just torn his shirt in two different pieces, and she had no idea why.

But Aleksander's face was contorted with a mournful expression. Tears were fully flowing out uninhibited. This was not a state that Aleksander would show lightly.

"I *do* love you, Liliana!" He proclaimed loudly in a sobbing voice. "I love you with all of my heart!" With that, the boy began weeping. "I don't want to go! I want to stay with you! I would love to take your offer and live here! I cherish the idea of marrying you! But I cannot abandon my father to die!"

Aleksander fell to his knees, still weeping.

All of Liliana's anger quickly vanished away at that sight. She walked up to him and knelt in the dirt beside him. There, the two embraced, and both of them cried together.

Once both had sufficiently recovered, Aleksander looked straight into Liliana's eyes.

"I love you, Liliana Hodor," he asserted firmly. "And I am going to make a vow to you today."

Aleksander then quickly began removing his shoes. Liliana wiped her eyes as she pondered what Aleksander was doing. Then, taking one shoe in both of his hands, Aleksander ripped it apart into two separate chunks. He did this in one fluid movement.

"What are you doing? And just how strong *are* you?" Liliana marveled, very confused.

Aleksander did the same with his other shoe. "It's from my culture. We call it a covenant, which means 'to cut.' When a very solemn promise is made, you're supposed to walk between two halves of animal carcasses. I don't have any animals to divide, so I hope my shoes will suffice for you."

Liliana wasn't sure how to answer that. But, as she watched, Aleksander placed the halves of his shoes apart from one another and walked through them.

"Liliana Hodor," he declared to her, "I vow to you before God Almighty that, though I am leaving for America, I will one day return here. I will come back to you, take you up in my arms, and marry you, should you still wish it. I will love you endlessly and do everything in my power to make you the happiest bride on this Earth. Should I not fulfill this vow, let this happen to me." Aleksander then gestured back to

116

the ripped shoes that he just walked through.

"This is very morbid," Liliana couldn't help but think. However, she knew Aleksander was doing it to assure her not only of his love but that he was serious in every fiber of his being about his intention to wed her.

"Of course, if one of us dies, I will be free of this vow," Aleksander disclaimed. "Other than that, I will fulfill the covenant that I have made with you this day."

Liliana was convinced. The two gave each other solemn promises that they would remain faithful to each other and wait until the day that Aleksander could raise enough funds to return to Zaginiony and take Liliana as his bride. They embraced once more before Aleksander departed. Tears were shed once more as the two young people knew it would be years before they would see each other again. Little did they know that more tears were being shed by another individual: Tomasz Kurtz.

Tomasz had just sold his house, gathering what other funds he could before their big move, when he saw Aleksander returning. The boy had his shirt torn and was walking barefoot. His eyes looked sore from crying, and his head hung low.

And Tomasz began to cry, realizing that he had done this to his son. All the same, he was resolute in his decision. They were leaving for America.

CHAPTER ELEVEN:

Letters

Aleksander sat down to write his first letter to Liliana.

December 12, 1935

Dear Liliana,

The boy tapped his pencil several times on the table, finding himself at a loss for words. Speaking, he found difficult at times. Writing? A whole different story. At least in conversation, the other person could sometimes pick up the slack and help Aleksander out. When it came to writing a letter, Aleksander had the whole floor to himself. This was not to mean that Aleksander had nothing to say. No, he had quite a bit to say.

Quite a bit of unfortunate things to say...

Aleksander closed his eyes, took a deep breath, and reopened his eyes.

Then, he began to write:

I miss you. I hope you'll forgive me for taking so

long to write you. Things...have not gone as desired.

Aleksander glanced over at his father, who was sleeping less than a meter from the table Aleksander was writing on. The "house" they were able to afford

118

could barely be called a shack, but it was among the only options they had as poor immigrants in a struggling country. Aleksander wished to write happier things, but he did not want to lie to Liliana. With a small chuckle, Aleksander thought their misfortune might make Liliana slightly happier than if they had been doing incredibly well.

My father was under the impression that America was thriving due to a letter from my aunt. He was mistaken, however. America is going through a depression, much like the rest of Europe.

We have discovered that my aunt is no longer with us but passed away near the beginning of this Great Depression due to starvation. At least, that is what we were told by individuals who lived in her area. We found no grave, nor my uncle. We were told my uncle traveled west after her death to try and find a better life. I pray he has found one.

As for my father and me, we have found ourselves in quite a difficult circumstance, but we have lodged among other Polish immigrants who are helping us learn the English language. It's frightfully confusing,

but I suppose all new languages are.

Aleksander took a moment to gather his thoughts. He did not want this letter to be completely dismal, but as he paused, staring up at the leaking ceiling of their shack, he realized there weren't many happy things to write about. On top of that, he was tired. It was past midnight, but this was the only time he could write his letter to Liliana. Their poverty demanded that Aleksander work as much as possible. Schooling was no longer an option.

Aleksander rubbed his eyes before thinking of how he could elaborate on the job situation and swing it into a positive light.

Everyone in New York is looking for work, looking

for jobs. The only reason I'm able to secure some

work is because of my strength and work ethic.

Father frantically tried to get some work as well, but

his ailments made it impossible. No employer would

take in a man who coughed like he was at death's

door. No, with his condition, Father is guaranteed to

stay at home. However, we've made the best of it.

While I work, Father studies to try and be a teacher to me. He hates math so much, but reads with the other Poles around here to get a grasp on it so he can teach it to me. I really admire that about him. He's also learning the language much faster than I am, so I rely on him heavily for that. It's a good system we've worked out. God is still taking care of us, even though I—

Aleksander stopped writing. He was about to say, "Even though I believe it wasn't the Lord's will to come here."

He thought over that statement for a while. Would writing that be dishonoring his father? Would it lower Liliana's respect for Tomasz?

He pondered on that for a great while. He loved and respected his father highly. Even though he disagreed with Tomasz's decision throughout their move to America, he wanted to be obedient and honor him.

After a great deal of thought, Aleksander continued with his letter. It was not dishonoring to tell the truth.

God is still taking care of us, even though I believe

it wasn't the Lord's will to come here, and though I say that, I'm not bitter at my father at all. He did what he thought was best, and sometimes what we think is best is a wrong turn. All the same, glory goes to Jesus for providing for us in the midst of this hard time.

It may take me longer to get back to Zaginiony. All of the money I make is completely gone, almost hours after I am paid. It's what has to be done for now, but I will not break my vow. I will return to you, my Liliana.

I love you. I cannot wait to see you. I hope you are doing much better than we are.

Sincerely,

Your Aleksander

Aleksander then quietly got into the old bed he and his father shared and very quickly passed into sleep.

January 24, 1936

Dear Aleksander,

I miss you as well. I have to confess that I am still angry with you, in part. Well, that's not entirely true. I fluctuate. There are days when I thank God that we are still able to be promised to each other, even though you're so far away. Days when I know in my heart that you will indeed come and finally marry me.

There are, however, other days when I am absolutely livid with you for how you decided to go to such a country. A depression? Are you serious? Your father didn't think to look into that before leaving? He really just dove head-first into shallow waters, didn't he?

Forgive me, I don't mean to belittle him. I just need you back. I need you with me. What if something happens to you? Knowing you, you're working like a dog. Please don't work yourself to death. Oh, Aleksander, is there **anything** I can do or say to get you to come back home? My father is still wealthy.

We can pay for a trip back. Please, take the offer.

Convince your father. Lie to him if you have to. It will be better if you come back, I promise. How long do you think we will have to wait otherwise? A year? Two years? Ten years? Of course, I'll still wait for you. I will wait an eternity for you. But, I mean, don't make me have to if it's not necessary!

I hate to say it, but I will respect your decision if you don't take my offer. It was wrong of me to ask you to lie to your father. Don't do that. God would not be pleased, and I want our marriage to be perfectly in His will. I hope you understand my longing for you, though. I hope you long for me in the same way.

As for me, things feel like they've gone on the same way they always have. Nothing much has changed. Well, a few things have. Piotr is trying to catch my attention again. I told him there was a better chance for Russia to willingly give up Moscow to Poland. He understood the message and hasn't tried again since.

Oh, and there's a new girl in Zaginiony. She moved here from Germany. It's quite eerie because she and I look very similar. People keep getting us confused. Her name is Hannah, which also doesn't sound too different from my own name. And guess what? She's Jewish, like you. Once I found that out, I said "Shalom" to her, and she was so moved! She looked frightened at first, like I had just discovered a terrible secret about her, but once I told her that I was courting a Jewish boy, she seemed extremely delighted.

She told me how some people in Germany were not so fond of Jewish people, and she didn't want me spreading it around to others. I asked her if it was permissible for me to tell you, and she said it was fine.

If you get a chance, do you think you could send a photograph of yourself with your next letter? If it costs too much money, don't worry about it. I just wish to see your face again. I've sent a photo of myself with this letter, in case you wanted to see my face.

    I love you, Aleksander. Please be safe. I pray for you daily. Please come home soon.

    Love,

        Your Liliana

    This correspondence carried on for years, much to both of the young people's misery. They didn't want to just send letters to one another, but to be able to see each other with their own eyes. To hold each other close. To hear each other's voice. But things are not always within our control, though we sometimes pretend they are.

    For something was coming that would completely upset both Liliana's and Aleksander's plans.

CHAPTER TWELVE:

1939

Four years. Liliana was both aggravated and utterly miserable at just those two words. Four years. It had been four years since she had seen Aleksander Kurtz. She spoke with him, of course. They sent letters as often as they were both able. For Aleksander, he seemed to have much less free time than she did, which made perfect sense. The poor boy was frequently doing hard labor, taking care of his sickly father, as well as learning American schooling from that same father.

Liliana sighed, rereading Aleksander's last letter that came back at the very end of July. She sighed again, folding the letter back up as she yearned not to read Aleksander's words but to hear them.

As much as she wished, though, that would not change anything. She had to trust that Aleksander would keep his promise. For now, it was best to focus on what was instead of what would be. Liliana checked the time and wondered when Hannah would return. Liliana sighed when she found that she wouldn't return for another six hours.

"Poor girl," Liliana thought as she recalled how Hannah had arrived in Zaginiony. She often uttered those words, most of the time when Hannah came to mind. Hannah was an eighteen-year-old, only two years younger than Liliana. When she first came to

Zaginiony, she knew very little Polish, she was destitute, and she was alone.

Thankfully, Liliana had learned German in some out-of-school tutoring. Her parents had thought it wise, considering Germany was not only their neighbor, but the border was incredibly close to Zaginiony. Liliana had acted as interpreter for Hannah once it was clear that she struggled greatly with Polish. Hannah had stated that her family was attacked, and she was forced to run away from her home. Liliana had found it rather odd when she left out a great deal of details, but figured it was simply due to the poor girl being traumatized, sick, and frighteningly thin.

She likely did not want to go into too many details of all that had happened to her and her family.

After some discussion among her family and some other townsfolk of Zaginiony, Liliana told Hannah they could live with the Hodors. Hannah was overwhelmed by such kindness and promised not to be a burden. She quickly tried to find work and was able to secure a job in Danzig. Thinking it too much to ask, Hannah was found walking to work before dawn in order to travel the twenty-four kilometers in time for her shift. Once the Hodors found out, they called upon Mr. Kowalski to see if he would loan her a horse to ride into town.

Mr. Kowalski was an old farmer who, in his later years, found a hobby in collecting horses. His grown children worked the fields, and Mr. Kowalski found himself idle. So, he started taking in and purchasing extra horses, finding that caring for them was both pleasurable and good for getting his old joints moving. Furthermore, he was more than happy to loan a horse to Hannah for travel, and Feliks in Danzig was equally content to hold onto the horse until Hannah finished her shift.

Some time passed, and Liliana discovered more about Hannah than she had intended. She was a remarkable girl in all areas save one: she was horribly untidy when it came to her living quarters. The spare bedroom that she was living in was worse than a pigsty. Wondering to herself how anyone could live like this, Liliana began tidying up the room. As she did, she came across a necklace that had the Star of David on it. A Jewish emblem. Being reminded of her beloved, Liliana was delighted to know that she had met another Jewish person. She couldn't wait to say "Shalom, shalom" when Hannah returned from work that day. But what a reaction Liliana was met with! Hannah responded with her face going pale and her eyes bulging wide. She became incredibly fearful of Liliana for those few moments after those two simple words. Thankfully, Hannah was set at ease after Liliana gave her explanation.

Then it was Hannah's turn to give hers.

Hannah's family was attacked by a group of antisemitic young men back in Germany. Since Hitler had come into power, he was swaying the people of Germany against the Jewish population. First, it started simply with separation. Later, it came with violence. The Jewish people were being wrongfully blamed for most of the problems that had been going on in Germany. Even some of the churches were siding with Hitler after he made the argument that the Jewish people were the ones who crucified Jesus and were therefore forsaken by God.

Liliana was horrified to hear of some of the treatment the German people had brought upon the Jews. Things had escalated worse and worse until Hannah's parents were beaten to death by a group of thugs.

It was why Hannah had run to Poland, concealing her heritage much like Esther had. However, she trusted Liliana enough to confide this, but asked her not to tell anyone else.

"Poor girl," Liliana thought again after recalling the events. She then glanced again at the clock. Only five minutes had passed.

"Best to do something more productive with my time," Liliana grumbled as she decided to head outside. "I'll go insane with impatience at this rate."

But as she headed outside, she thought she heard an odd sound off in the distance. It sounded like thunder, but there wasn't a cloud in the sky.

"Peculiar," Liliana muttered to herself.

But as she gazed up into the sky, she also noticed planes were flying from the west. Many planes.

This began to make Liliana nervous. What did this mean? She was suddenly interrupted by the sound of an approaching horse.

It was Hannah!

"Hannah?" Liliana called. "Aren't you supposed to be in—"

"*Schnell!*" Hannah screamed as she raced her horse towards Liliana.

Liliana was startled by this. Hannah was speaking in her native German. She had been studying Polish under Liliana for four years now and was essentially fluent.

Reverting back to German, accompanied by all the other oddities that were simultaneously happening, made Liliana realize that something bad was taking place.

Finally reaching Liliana near the front of her house, Hannah attempted to leap off the horse as she reined the animal in. This ended very poorly, for Hannah's foot got caught in one of the stirrups, and she promptly fell into the dirt next to the horse.

"Hannah!" Liliana cried, running to her and the horse. First, grabbing the horse and trying to calm it in order to keep it from inadvertently stepping on Hannah.

"Hannah, are you all right?!" Liliana turned to the girl who was on the ground, but as she looked at her, she was frantically trying to scramble up off the ground.

"*Wir müssen rennen! Wir müssen uns verstecken!*" She cried out.

"Slow down, Hannah!" Liliana told her, releasing the horse and following after Hannah. "Either slow down or speak Polish! What's going on?!"

Hannah turned to Liliana and seized her by the

shoulders. Her face was etched with fright.

"They're coming," she panted to Liliana. "I saw them in Danzig. They're attacking. Liliana, they're taking Poland."

"Who?"

"Who else?" Hannah shuddered as tears were building up in her eyes. "Hitler and his dogs."

Suddenly, a loud boom could be heard several kilometers off. Then, the sound of a tank shell came whistling overhead. Before the two girls knew it, the Hodor estate behind them, being the largest and most exemplary building in Zaginiony, erupted in a fiery explosion.

Aleksander sauntered into the small shack that he called home after another grueling day at work. He tried to think positively, noting that his savings were finally starting to climb to a substantial sum. The journey back to Poland was looking more and more like a possibility rather than just a hopeless fantasy. All the same, he was *tired*, and it was easy to fall into the rut of wishing for something better and easier.

"Aleksander," His father greeted him as he entered. This was typical, but Aleksander paused and focused his eyes on Tomasz. Tomasz had said his name in a certain tone.

One of worry and gravity.

As Aleksander gazed at his father, he found that his father was pointing at the radio. Aleksander had generally ignored the radio. Tomasz kept it on quite often, wanting to know of news that was happening, particularly in Europe. Sometimes, Tomasz stayed up late, listening to the radio when Aleksander wished to sleep. Hence, Aleksander got accustomed to tuning it out. So, when Aleksander had come back home, he hadn't even realized the radio was on. But as he began listening, his breath left him altogether:

> "Up to the very last, it would have been quite possible to have arranged a peaceful and honorable settlement between Germany and Poland, but Hitler would not have it. He had evidently made up his mind to attack Poland whatever happened, and although He now says he put forward reasonable proposals which were rejected by the Poles, that is not a true statement. The proposals were never shown to the Poles, nor to us, and, although they were announced in a German broadcast on Thursday night, Hitler did not wait to hear comments on them but ordered his troops to cross the Polish frontier the next morning. His action shows convincingly that there is no chance of expecting

that this man will ever give up
his practice of using force to
gain his will. He can only be
stopped by force.

"We and France are today, in
fulfillment of our obligations,
going to the aid of Poland, who
is so bravely resisting this
wicked and unprovoked attack on
her people. We have a clear
conscience. We have done all
that any country could do to
establish peace. The situation
in which no word given by
Germany's ruler could be
trusted and no people or
country could feel themselves
safe has become intolerable.
And now that we have resolved
to finish it, I know that you
will all play your part with
calmness and courage."

"What has happened, Father?" Aleksander uttered
quietly. He had heard the words. He had understood
them. He had no issue comprehending what the
broadcast had declared.

He simply could not believe it. It had to be some
sort of misunderstanding. Knowing his father would
not lie to him, he had to ask him.

"What has happened?" Aleksander asked again.

"That was Neville Chamberlain, the prime minister of the United Kingdom," Tomasz murmured slowly and sadly. "And, son…Hitler has invaded Poland. Starting at Danzig." Trembling, Aleksander's legs buckled, and he fell to his knees. Danzig was only fifteen miles from Zaginiony.

More importantly, it was fifteen miles from the woman to whom his heart belonged.

CHAPTER THIRTEEN:
A Regretful Discussion

Tomasz watched Aleksander's reaction. The boy seemed to be in shock as he sat on his knees, staring blankly at their radio. With a heavy sigh, Tomasz was overwhelmed with guilt, but at that moment, he resolved to right his wrongs. Tomasz slowly picked himself off his bed, coughing as he did so. Aleksander didn't notice, nor did he notice when Tomasz actually left their tiny house.

As Tomasz walked out in the night, he reflected on how warm it was for September. He didn't like it. The weather shouldn't have been in the mid-70s in September. But as he hobbled along, he shook his head. Why was he thinking about the weather after what he had just heard? His home nation was at war with a madman. All of the people he knew back in Poland were being invaded, likely scrambling for their lives to get away from Hitler's butchers. At that thought, he stopped walking for a moment. He took a shaky breath and let out some pent-up coughs. He gripped his chest as he did so. His lungs burned, and he knew he was getting worse at a much quicker rate now. How much time did he have left? He couldn't say, but he knew it wouldn't be more than five years. Most likely much less than that. He nodded to himself as he gazed up at the sky.

"And we know that all things work together for

good to them that love God, to them who are the called according to His purpose." Tomasz quoted Romans 8:28. "…I'm sorry, Lord. I didn't look to You when I should have. I was proud and afraid. And I believe I will pay the consequence of that. However, please help me swallow my pride now. Give me the strength to help my boy."

With that short prayer, Tomasz proceeded to go to his neighbors.

Tomasz and Aleksander lived in a Hooverville just outside New York City. Everyone was packed tightly together in shanties made of tin, cardboard, lumber, tar paper, glass, or whatever other materials people could salvage. Tomasz knew where all of the Polish ones lived, but he wasn't aiming at just the Polish. He was going to speak to everyone. Over the four years he had lived in America, he had built up quite a relationship with many of the people they lived around.

Though he didn't have the strength he would like, he had practical knowledge that assisted with many of his neighbors' troubles. He would instruct younger men how to construct their shanty so they could make the most of what they had. He gave advice to those who were looking for work as to where to look and how to catch the eyes of employers. After he learned English, he even began teaching what he knew to others who were still struggling with the language. His most passionate pastime was holding a Bible study and prayer time for anyone who wanted to come. Due to all of this, he had set up quite a reputation. He was known by many as a principled Christian man who wouldn't ask for help from any but would freely give out help where he could.

Until today.

Reaching a small gathering of fellows who were shooting the breeze, Tomasz took off his cap as he approached them. Seeing him, the men quickly hushed, and all turned to face him.

Tomasz appeared meek and humble before them, adorned with a sad, tired face.

"I need your help," he murmured. "My boy needs money."

No further explanation was given, though Tomasz was prepared to give it. Before he opened his mouth to tell them more, he found that they were already taking what loose change they had and offering it to him. As far as they were concerned, Tomasz didn't need to explain.

Saying that his son needed money was enough, for not only did Tomasz have a great reputation among them, but Aleksander did as well. Even though he was fairly successful at finding work due to his work ethic and strength, he often came off work ready to help his neighbors. He did heavy lifting for many who were too old or crippled to do it themselves. He helped build some of the shanties so that the wind and cold were kept out during the winter. He had done his fair share of helping this little community he was in. Both Tomasz and Aleksander had helped, neither of them ever asking for help in return. So, when these men heard Tomasz ask for money to help Aleksander, they gave it without hesitation. As Tomasz went about the Hooverville, he kept finding this to be the case. The women were exceptionally giving, even the ones who had little ones to provide for. It cemented in Tomasz's heart that God was with him and was putting His blessing upon the idea that Tomasz had.

In a few hours, Tomasz returned to his home.

Aleksander was found praying in the corner, to which Tomasz smiled inwardly. Despite all his faults, Tomasz seemed to have raised his son to look to the Lord.

Tomasz waited patiently for his son to finish praying. When Aleksander was done, he almost seemed startled to see Tomasz standing there.

"Father, I—" he stood up and began to say. Tomasz held up his hand, silencing Aleksander.

"I will let you speak, but please let me speak first," he told his son.

Then, Tomasz knelt on the ground before his son.

"I have failed you," Tomasz began, tears moistening his eyes. "I would even go so far as to say that I sinned against you, my son."

"Father—"

"Please let me finish," Tomasz interrupted. "I have portrayed an ill example of what a Christian man ought to be. I have been a hypocrite, and I hope you will forgive me for it."

Tomasz sighed, looking up at his son.

"I did not ask counsel of the Lord before deciding to come here," Tomasz confessed. "I relied on my stubbornness, pride, and fear rather than relying on God. It is my fault that we have come to a poverty-stricken land where you have had to work four times as hard as you would have had I taken help from Feliks or even the Hodors. I am sorry." Standing to his feet, Tomasz looked his boy in the eye. "Can you forgive your flawed father?"

Aleksander immediately embraced Tomasz. "Of course, Father. I already knew all of this, but I was never angry with you. I have already forgiven you."

Tomasz was tempted to let forth even more tears now, but he refrained.

"Thank you, son," Tomasz replied, his voice being somewhat choked up. "Though, I will say that I'm happy we weren't in Poland when the Germans invaded. Else, I know you would have been bold enough to fight back, and I doubt that even you could have overcome an invasion." Then, stepping away from Aleksander, Tomasz held out the money he had collected from the community.

Aleksander stared at it. For the Hooverville they were living in, it looked to be quite a large sum.

"Regardless, I think we both know what needs to be done now," Tomasz told Aleksander.

Aleksander stared at the money and then stared at his father. "What do you mean?"

"I know you would go to the ends of the Earth for that Hodor girl," Tomasz said. "This will make it a little easier to get there."

"What are you talking about?" Aleksander stuttered. "Where did you even get all of that?"

"Our neighbors," Tomasz explained. "They were more than willing to give what they had to help you out. You need to go get your Liliana, Aleksander. Save her. Save anyone you can in Zaginiony."

"I would," Aleksander affirmed as he continually stared at his father. "…But you."

"Don't worry about me," Tomasz told him. "It's time to leave your father and cling to the woman who will be your wife."

"I'm your only source of income." Aleksander persisted. "You can't get work in your condition. Without me, you'll—"

Tomasz put his hands on his son's shoulder. "My fate, whether I have you to take care of me or not, is in the Lord's hands. My condition is worsening anyway. I may die tomorrow, son. You have honored me throughout your life, and I am so proud of you. But now, it's time to let me go. One day, we will see each other again in the Lord's presence, but for now, you are needed more urgently elsewhere."

Aleksander knew that his father was right, as hard as it was to simply leave his father behind. It felt like he was abandoning his only family. He was well aware that Tomasz would likely die without him around.

Still, Aleksander knew, from the moment he heard that radio broadcast, that he was going to go back to Zaginiony to retrieve Liliana and anyone else he could. The Lord simply confirmed it with Tomasz's words and the money. So, Aleksander left, bidding his father a bitter farewell.

Using the majority of his savings, in addition to the money he had received from Tomasz, he was able to buy a one-way trip through Pan American to cross the ocean back to Europe.

CHAPTER FOURTEEN:

Crossing The Border

September 7th. Six days after the initial invasion of Danzig. Four days after Aleksander heard about the invasion. Two days after Zaginiony was invaded, though Aleksander wasn't aware of that. He was happy to have gotten so far in so little time, but he knew that time was against him. He knew that it could already be far too late. He knew little of Germany and her politics. He had very little understanding as to why Hitler would command the invasion of a nation that posed no threat to him, but Aleksander didn't have to understand why; all he needed to understand was that it was happening.

"Where Germany goes, Russia will follow. Be wary of the Soviets." Some of Tomasz's final words to Aleksander rang in his head. Aleksander pondered on this as he tried to make an escape route. Believing wholeheartedly that he would be able to arrive in Zaginiony and rescue the townspeople, he began thinking about where they would need to flee. West would be impossible because of Germany.

East would be as well if Tomasz's suspicions were correct. That left either north or south. North would be the shortest distance, but it would also be extremely difficult. In order to get out of Poland through the north, they would either need to travel northeast through Prussia or get a boat to get them to

Sweden. Prussia was out of the question since it belonged to Germany, and hiring a boat out of German-occupied Danzig was unfathomable.

Aleksander gave a heavy sigh as he realized they would need to flee south. It would be a long and arduous journey, but if they could make it to neutral Czechoslovakia or Romania, they might just be safe. Romania would be best, he noted, due to the Germans pushing in from the west. It would be best to move east to avoid being caught by them. Sighing again, Aleksander realized he had chosen the path that required the most travel through a country that was being invaded. It would be so incredibly dangerous. All the while, he would likely have all manner of people with him. From toddlers to the elderly.

"I need to pray again," Aleksander concluded. *"It will only be by God's miraculous grace that we make it through this."*

And so, Aleksander knelt and prayed.

The skipper eyed this strange American as he knelt on the bow again. The American had done this several times throughout their small voyage. The skipper was a young, Swedish man by the name of Rolf who was trying to start up his fishing business. Herring and Sprat were plentiful in the Baltic Sea, and fishing was a promising career. Rolf was even able to finally purchase his own fishing boat, but for the life of him, he was struggling to have anyone come and help him.

Commercial fishing was not a one-man job.

144

Hiring employees had proven harder than he had thought, and he needed money. Then this American approached him, offering up a good amount of cash in order to take him from Trelleborg, Sweden, to Danzig, Poland. Rolf knew what was happening down in Poland. The last thing he wanted to do was get shot at, but the American was waving so much in front of his face that it was very hard to ignore. The United States dollar had been tied to the *krona* just a month ago. One U.S. dollar was worth over four *kronor*. That meant that whatever this American thought he was paying Rolf, it was actually four times that. So, despite his better judgment, Rolf took the money and allowed the American aboard his small fishing vessel.

Since then, the American hadn't done anything but wait on the front of the bow, ever looking out in the dark night and kneeling down every now and again.

Rolf shrugged to himself. Whatever the American was doing was his business. The boat ride was almost halfway over. They had almost covered four hours' worth of travel and were nearing Poland's shores. They would soon be able to see the Peninsula of Hel. Beyond that, it was just twenty kilometers to Danzig. True, Rolf would have to travel all the way back to Trelleborg, but the American had paid more than enough to make it worth it. Rolf then glanced around him at the waters of the Baltic Sea. It was a peaceful night. Warmer than Rolf would have liked. It was his opinion that there seemed to be a heat wave going on recently. Maybe summer's last burst before autumn took the reins.

Then, as Hel began to come into view, Rolf spotted a black shadow. He shivered as he realized he was staring at nothing less than a German destroyer that was waiting inside Danzig Bay. Acting quickly, Rolf cut the engine, halting the fishing boat in the water.

Getting any closer could risk being spotted. Rolf realized that he very easily could have been shot at. His boat could have been blown out of the water. He might even lose his life tonight.

This was not worth the money.

"American," Rolf spoke anxiously in English as he walked out to the bow. The American was already staring at him with a questioning look. He had been doing so since Rolf stopped the boat.

Rolf swallowed nervously as he dug the American money out of his pockets. He took a third of it for himself and held out the rest to Aleksander. Aleksander glanced at the money, an angry look overcoming his face.

"I'm sorry," Rolf apologized. "I can't do it. I'm not about to risk my life for this. You shouldn't either. It's suicide. I'll return all but a third of the money, and I'll even take you back to Trelleborg for free. But no closer. Please." Aleksander's face softened as he witnessed the evident fear on Rolf's face. He took the money from Rolf's hand, and Rolf sighed with relief. Aleksander then counted through the money and held part of it out to him.

Rolf was rather confused by this. "No, I said I'll take you back for free."

"You've earned it, sir," Aleksander replied in English, giving a small smile.

Rolf hesitantly took the portion back as Aleksander placed the remainder of his money in his pocket.

"Safe travels," Aleksander wished.

"Pardon?" Rolf stuttered, but it was too late to stop him. Rolf watched as Aleksander took a running start and leaped over the side of the boat, plunging into the dark waters of the Baltic Sea.

"You madman!" Rolf yelled over the side. "It's a twenty-four-kilometer swim to Danzig from here!"

But the American showed no intention of returning to the boat. He was swimming the front crawl stroke towards Poland.

"Americans," Rolf muttered in Swedish, shaking his head. "Think they can do anything."

Aleksander emerged from the cold waters, finally on the shores of Danzig. His physical exhaustion felt absolute as he simply struggled to stand. Aleksander had a newfound respect for the individuals he had heard of, who had swum great lengths, like the English Channel and other places like that. He told himself as he finally stood up on trembling legs that he would never do something like that again. He knew that he had almost drowned more than a few times due to fatigue, but the Lord had given him some extra strength that night in order to make the fifteen-mile swim.

He tried taking a step forward but found it too much for his right leg. It collapsed under him, and he fell face-first in the sand. Breathing heavily, Aleksander made a *"tch"* sound as he tried to push himself to stand once more. He knew that he couldn't stay on the beach for very long. It was one thing to swim past a destroyer without being noticed, but even in the dark, he could easily be spotted against the light-colored beach. He pushed himself up to stand again when he suddenly heard something.

"Du da drüben! Bleib, wo du bist!"

Aleksander began to panic. It was clearly German language. This couldn't be how it ended. He had gotten so far in so little time! Traveling from America to Sweden to Poland itself in less than a week! Now, to be stopped here? When he was only fifteen miles away from Liliana?

"Please, Lord," Aleksander prayed as he sat up to his knees. *"Please don't let me be stopped here."*

Two German soldiers ran up to him, one pointing a rifle at him. The other, drawing close and examining him. They looked at one another before the first soldier began speaking rapid German to him. Aleksander never learned German, even though they lived so close. He didn't see it as vital. Now, he regretted that slightly. He thought he might be able to convince them of some lie if he understood anything they said.

The Germans both paused, the realization

148

dawning on them that Aleksander understood nothing of what they said.

"Maybe one of them understands Polish?" Aleksander thought to himself. *"It's worth a shot."*

He opened his mouth but was stopped when he heard a third individual.

"Guten abend, soldaten," A voice spoke from behind the German soldiers. Both soldiers spun around to find an old man approaching.

"Oh!" The old man laughed nervously, putting up his hands to show he had no weapons. He then began speaking gently to the two soldiers in German.

As he spoke, Aleksander realized that the old man was none other than Feliks. Feliks had come to his rescue. Looking harmless and kind, Feliks seemed to be reasoning with the soldiers while gesturing to Aleksander. Aleksander wished he could follow what Feliks was telling them, so he could play along with whatever fabrication Feliks was weaving with his words. However, Aleksander was given his clue when Feliks ever so subtly said "American" while pointing to Aleksander.

"Of course," Aleksander thought.

"Sorry, Uncle," Aleksander spoke in English, trying his best to imitate the American accent. "I really shouldn't have had that third beer. I have no idea where I am right now, and why do these guys have ***guns?"***

Feliks tried his best to suppress a smile as he gave a slight wink to Aleksander. Evidently, it was just the push that the German soldiers needed to confirm

149

Feliks' story. The two soldiers looked at one another. Killing or capturing an American could have been very hazardous. Germany was currently at war with Poland, France, and the United Kingdom. Dragging America into this conflict was not at all wise right now. Furthermore, they both knew that they would get blamed for it. So, allowing the old man to take his "nephew" home, the two German soldiers pretended that they didn't see anything.

As Feliks helped Aleksander up and began hobbling away in the direction of Feliks' house, Feliks asked Aleksander under his breath, "How did you know I told them that you were drunk?"

"I didn't," Aleksander responded, "but it was the only thing that made sense for me to be swimming out here in the dead of night. And I bet my walk is really selling it right now."

"How did you know I was coming?" Aleksander asked Feliks as they arrived back at Feliks' house.

"I just so happened to be keeping my sights on that German destroyer in the bay..." Feliks mentioned as he messed with food in his kitchen. "I'm trying to keep quiet in the brush next to the beach, noting all the information I can gather when, lo and behold, I spot a figure swimming past that big boat. Even with the binoculars, it was hard to discern that it was you. But when you crawled onto that beach, there was no mistaking it." Feliks then gave an irritated glare to Aleksander from the kitchen. "The foolhardy son of Tomasz has put himself directly in a war zone."

"But…why were you spying on the German destroyer?" Aleksander inquired.

"I'm a spy, child," Feliks scoffed. "It's what I do."

"Still?" Aleksander marveled. "Who do you report to?"

"Enough questions." Feliks scolded Aleksander as he gave him some food to eat. "After you eat this, you go straight to bed. You need to recover your strength."

"I'm far too worked up to sleep," Aleksander responded. "You know why I'm here, right?"

Feliks paused after he gave Aleksander a large glass of water. "Yes, I know why you're here. And it's foolish."

"Foolish to try and save Liliana?" Aleksander asked with a breath of heat. "Foolish to help innocent people in Zaginiony?"

"Yes, boy," Feliks affirmed. "You don't understand what kind of operation is being executed. Poland is going to be overrun. Millions of people are going to be killed."

"All the more to escape while we have the chance," Aleksander argued. "I know that God has guided my way. He has called me for this mission, else I would not have gotten this far with such ease."

"Ease, you say?" Feliks scoffed. "You almost died there on a beach."

"But I didn't," Aleksander persisted. "Because you were there. You were at the right place at the right time to save me. The Lord intended that. You

151

must see how just my being here is miraculous. I believe He will make the rest of this mission the same way. I am going to Zaginiony. It's far too late to turn back now, nor would I do so even if you ordered me to."

Feliks sighed. "There's that stubbornness I've seen from your father...But I can't argue that it does indeed appear that you are being led by Christ's divine hand. What is your plan at this point?"

Aleksander hesitated. "I...I don't entirely know. Some information, if you have any, would be very beneficial." Feliks nodded as he sat down next to Aleksander.

"Listen well," he told the young man. "This is what I know. When the Germans took Danzig, they had a pruning process. Anyone who was regarded as a threat was eliminated. They have a list of those who need to be killed. Usually, people of prominence or influence, like scholars, officers, or members of the clergy. They divide up the people into those who are deemed worthy of death and those who are allowed to live. The ones they are going to kill are simply taken out of town, shot, and buried, whether they are dead or not. The rest? Many have been taken away, and I doubt they're taking us to a vacation resort."

Aleksander's eyes widened. "'Taking us'?"

Feliks nodded slowly. "They're coming for me, too. I perceive they'll find out about my Jewish heritage soon. I'm likely destined for..."

He was about to finish, but thought it better not to

152

bring up the death camps to young Aleksander.

"I'll be fine," he muttered instead.

"You should come with me!" Aleksander pressed.

"No, I will not," Feliks declared adamantly. "I will undoubtedly slow you down. I am *old,* Aleksander. Riding the way you need to is far behind me. And the journey ahead of you is too much for me. I accept my fate and will face it with dignity."

Aleksander was about to argue further, but Feliks gave him a hard stare. It was enough to silence the boy. He had seen that look many times from his father and was well-acquainted with it enough to know that it meant the subject would not be discussed further.

"What I can do for you now is provide you with horses," Feliks added further, "and a gun. Only one, however. It's all I have left after they went through my things."

"That will be more than enough." Aleksander bowed his head in gratitude.

Feliks patted the boy's head. "You need to rest. You should ride out tomorrow evening. Don't go into the town until nightfall. Get your girl and then get yourself out of Poland."

CHAPTER FIFTEEN:

The Selection

The sun was setting on Zaginiony on September 8th.

Much had changed in just three simple days. The *Wehrmacht* had charged in with a few tanks, but most were simple soldiers of the German army. Zaginiony surrendered without any resistance whatsoever. They had no militia. Even if they had, it would be insurmountable odds against the strength of the *Wehrmacht* that came against them. The town itself was no bigger than four square kilometers. The largest building happened to be the Hodor's house, which was destroyed by a tank shell. Next to that, the next largest building was the church. Aside from the school, the rest of the town was made up of simple houses.

With such an easy victory over such a small town, most of the *Wehrmacht* continued on their march further into Poland. Only a platoon of soldiers was left to take care of the inhabitants of Zaginiony. They were under the command of *Oberleutnant* Hoffmann, who was very clear on what was to happen next. The influential were removed first: the sheriff, the pastor, Mr. Laris, and, to Liliana and Albin's horror, their parents. Jozef Hodor was not only incredibly wealthy but was also a man who was looked up to by all. That, combined with his military background, deemed him worthy of removal. He was quickly taken away. Upon discovering who his wife was, Hoffmann found it appropriate to have her die with her husband. Hoffmann wanted to make it clear that all of the townsfolk's lives hung in the balance of his choice and that it would be best for all of them to attempt to stay on his good side until the trucks arrived that would take them all away to labor camps.

Albin Hodor, however, cared very little for staying on Hoffmann's good side.

Albin had just turned fifteen years of age—a teenage boy full of strong emotions. Partnered with the grief and anger of losing his beloved parents, he decided to spout off some very un-Christian words directly at Hoffmann. Hoffmann, who could speak Polish, understood Albin perfectly.

In the town square, where everyone was gathered, Hoffmann promptly made a decision.

"Thank you for your honest opinions, young man," Hoffmann spoke to them all in Polish. Then, he snapped his fingers, and a *Wehrmacht* soldier ripped Albin away from his sister's arms.

"I wonder if anyone would share those opinions of yours if we thin out the herd a bit more," Hoffmann proclaimed loudly as he gestured for other soldiers to begin selecting Zaginiony inhabitants at random. They were all driven over to where Albin was. Hoffmann began listening with quiet pleasure as many of the townspeople began weeping, crying, and shouting in dismay. It was music to his ears.

"Take them away. You know what to do," he ordered a few of his men in German. His men did as they were told, pointing their rifles at the selection of Zaginiony inhabitants, ordering them to move. They slowly walked them out of town as their loved ones who stayed behind were weeping after them.

Hoffmann watched this display of despair with utmost contentment. The sister of the young man who had slandered him seemed to be the one who was crying out the most. Collapsing on her knees, her face was a contorted mess of anguish and sobbing.

Hoffmann smiled. Then, turning his eyes on the rest of the crowd, he was forced to do a double-take. There was a young woman near the back of the Zaginiony townsfolk who looked incredibly similar to the sister he was just watching. Looking between the two, he figured they were related. Sisters, perhaps. Possibly cousins. But as he speculated, he realized that the second girl was not acting like the rest of the people. She was, instead, wholly terrified. The other townspeople were frightened, yes, but Hoffmann could tell that this girl had a different kind of fear about her. A fear of knowledge. She trembled greatly, keeping her eyes down to the ground as if to avoid any eye contact. Hoffmann scratched his chin pensively. Perhaps he was simply overthinking things. Or perhaps...

He gestured to two of his soldiers to come closer and whispered something to each. The soldiers gave Hoffmann a confused, questioning look, but told Hoffmann that they would do as ordered. Hoffmann then approached the terrified girl as one of the soldiers began barking orders to the townsfolk, calling all of their attention.

The girl began shaking more vehemently as Hoffmann came closer to her. Hoffmann stood directly next to her, pulling out a cigarette and offering it to her.

"It will calm you," he spoke to her in Polish.

"No, thank you, sir," Hannah replied in Polish, still not making eye contact with him.

"Very well. By the way, I—" Hoffmann began but was interrupted.

One of his soldiers called, as if he were speaking to his fellow *Wehrmacht* soldiers, "Time to round up all of the Jews."

The thing was, he said this in the Hebrew language, as Hoffmann had told him the words. The Germans and Poles alike had no idea what the soldier said. The soldier himself had no idea what he said. But Hannah gasped in fright, fully understanding what the man said.

Then, her face had a whole new level of horrific panic upon it. For she realized that she had just given herself away. For the first time, she turned her eyes to look directly at *Oberleutnant* Hoffmann. He was grinning from ear to ear. "Got you." He whispered to her.

Albin allowed the tears to flow freely. He hadn't realized what he had done. Did he suspect that he

157

would be punished for shouting at Hoffmann? Of course, but he never considered that other people would be sentenced to death because of it. There had to be well over twenty people who were being marched alongside him. Just minutes ago, they were going to live. Now? Destined for death.

Because of **him**...

Albin just felt shocked at what was happening. He wasn't able to bring himself to say anything.

The soldiers cast them in the dirt outside town. Rifles were cocking all around and several whimpers and frightened cries were beginning to be heard.

At that moment, Albin's tears dried, and his anger revived. He hatefully glared at the invaders. He couldn't think of anything to say that felt right. Not that they would understand him anyway. But a glare of hatred and anger? That spoke plenty, and it was very easy to understand.

And they did understand.

As a result, one of the *Wehrmacht* soldiers stepped in front of him. He raised his rifle and pointed it directly at Albin's face.

Staring down the barrel of a rifle, Albin originally intended to angrily stare death in the face as he met his end. But as the soldier prepared to shoot, Albin found that he couldn't do it. His anger again melted away and was replaced with trembling fear.

He was about to die. He closed his eyes, so afraid of what was to happen next.

"Was ist das?!" German cries were suddenly heard.

A few gunshots started going off, causing many of the townsfolk of Zaginiony to shriek.

But the gunshots weren't aimed at them.

Albin opened his eyes to see the German soldier in front of him had his attention, like the rest of the soldiers, on a figure that was moving incredibly fast through the trees.

The figure ducked and weaved, moving close to the ground as the soldiers shot at it. Due to the darkness of the night, it was hard to tell what it was.

But whatever it was, it was there to kill.

It raised its hand and fired off multiple shots from a handgun. A few German soldiers were struck. Some cried out, while others silently collapsed to the ground and lay still. The other Germans who still stood continued to fire at it. The figure kept up its dodging dance, firing from its handgun until the handgun was out of ammo.

It ran up to the closest dead soldier and picked up the rifle that had fallen in the dirt. The figure slowed for just a second to retrieve the rifle. Albin squinted his eyes at it, trying to see what it was.

It was a man.

No, it was his sister's man! It was Aleksander Kurtz!

What in the world was he doing here?!

But there was no time for questions to be answered. Aleksander fired off several shots, nailing four of the ten remaining soldiers. One of which was the soldier standing directly in front of Albin.

But the six that remained now had an unmoving

target. They all began firing at Aleksander, forcing him to drop the weapon and flee behind several trees.

Then he was just…gone. Everything suddenly became silent.

The German soldiers were breathing heavily, exchanging glances with one another. They listened for any sound, watched for any movement.

Nothing.

Then, a rustling of leaves gained everyone's attention, German and Polish alike. One of the Polish prisoners was trying to make an escape! A teenage boy around Albin's age. The teenager had darted up from his crouched position, taking full advantage of the Germans being distracted, but he wasn't fast enough to disappear in the night. The closest German pointed his rifle at him, shouting loudly, but he never fired his gun. In fact, the soldier suddenly slumped, falling to the ground.

A knife was in his chest.

The five *Wehrmacht* soldiers who were left all gasped, glancing around frantically at where the knife had suddenly come from. This allowed the teenage boy to escape successfully. Other inhabitants of Zaginiony began looking at each other, silently wondering if they should try and make a run for it as well. Evidently, they weren't subtle about it, for the soldiers suddenly surrounded the townspeople, making no room for them to escape without alerting one of them. Each of the soldiers was looking outward from their little circle, making sure to be able to see all vantage points.

Once again, all was silent. No footsteps. No movement in the shadows. Only the sound of anxious breathing from both the *Wehrmacht* soldiers and the Zaginiony townspeople.

Albin began wondering if he truly did see Aleksander or if something else was at work here. It was dark out, so he easily could have misjudged the individual's face. Albin started considering that it could have been an angel sent from God to protect them from the devilish *Wehrmacht*. As he thought on this, something landed right next to him. It landed so softly that Albin thought it was a bird. But, as he glanced to his left, he saw a boot. Glancing up, he realized the figure that had been fighting the soldiers had magically manifested directly next to him. He was now in the center of the five *Wehrmacht* soldiers, yet all of the soldiers were facing away from him.

*"It **must** be an angel!"* Albin thought, completely convinced. How else would someone be able to simply appear out of nowhere like that?

All the same, the soldiers seemed to hear the soft landing as well. One turned to see what it was and was completely drained of color when he spotted the figure. He was small, yes, but he had appeared out of nowhere with barely a sound.

And his face…

A hollow, wide-eyed stare penetrated through the soldier. There was no mercy in those soulless eyes. Only a piercing, venomous gaze that overwhelmed the soldier with horrid dread.

The soldier was immediately persuaded that they were dealing with an otherworldly being. Still, he did his best to warn his comrades.

"Alarm!" The soldier barely squeaked out before the figure snatched his rifle and smashed the barrel of the weapon into his nose. As tears instantly flooded his eyes, his legs were swept out from under him, causing him to fall face-first into the dirt.

The other four soldiers swung around to find the figure in the midst of them.

But they were already too late, for he had the rifle aimed and was firing. Two of the soldiers fell to the ground as the Zaginiony townsfolk were screaming and ducking as low to the ground as they were able.

The figure turned the rifle to the next soldier. Pulling the trigger, the figure suddenly froze as all that happened was a *"click"* from the rifle.

He was out of ammunition. The two remaining *Wehrmacht* soldiers, still trying to get their own rifles in position, simultaneously grinned. There was no saving this strange man now.

They both aimed and fired, but found that both of their rifles made the exact same *"click"* sound.

They were out of ammunition as well. Now, it was their turn to freeze in a moment of panic, and that moment was all the figure needed. He leaped forward, vaulting over two Zaginiony inhabitants, took the rifle by the barrel, and swung the rifle like a bat at the first soldier. The butt of the gun made contact with the soldier's jaw, completely knocking him to the ground. Stealing the figure's idea, the second soldier took his rifle and plunged the butt of it right into the figure's face. The figure did nothing to dodge it.

He took it directly to his right cheek. The remarkable thing was that the figure was not knocked down like the other soldier had been. He was not even knocked back. There was no stagger, no recoil, not even a flinch. The figure took a powerful strike from a man much bigger than him and stopped the butt of the gun dead in its tracks… with his *face*.

The soldier's eyes widened, the rifle still pressed against the figure's cheek. The last thing that the soldier saw was the fierce, monstrous glare before the figure advanced upon him and took both his life as well as that of his fallen companion moments later.

Upon witnessing this, the German soldier who had his nose smashed got back up to his feet and began fleeing. He was not about to fight a devil or a wraith or whatever this man was. He did his best to sprint as fast away as he could, but stumbled over a fallen branch. The figure turned to see the soldier get back up and continue running. Moving briskly, the figure retrieved his knife from one of the dead soldiers and, after a second of aiming, expertly threw it right at the retreating soldier. Being struck directly in the spine, the soldier fell dead immediately.

The inhabitants of Zaginiony were frozen. Some with awe, some with sheer terror, many with both. They were all unsure of what to make of this man who just slew over a dozen *Wehrmacht* soldiers, some with his bare hands.

As they were debating whether or not to run from this new potential danger, the figure sighed and turned to them.

"Is anyone hurt?" He asked, his face etched with concern.

"It can't be," Albin was the first to speak back to the figure. "I thought I recognized you, but Aleksander...since when can you do all of *that?*"

With that revelation, the other townspeople of Zaginiony began recognizing him as well.

"Aleksander?"

"Tomasz's boy?"

"The Kurtz kid?"

He had changed. He had not exactly grown, for he was still the same size as he had been when he originally left for America with Tomasz. However, he had clearly aged, and not necessarily for the better. Hard labor in America seemed to have taken a toll on him. He looked much older than he should have. Not only that, but the man had not shaved in weeks. He had a full beard, masking much of the face that they were used to seeing when thinking of Aleksander.

At Albin's voice, Aleksander couldn't help but smile. "Albin Hodor, is that you?" Aleksander almost laughed. "You've grown!"

"More than you," Albin noted, Aleksander was now smaller than him. "Not that you need it. Do you realize all that you just did? What are you, made of stone? You took a rifle butt to the face without so much as flinching!" Aleksander's smile faded as he rubbed his cheek.

"That was unwise. It hurt tremendously. I think I'm bleeding." With that, he spat out some blood. "I think a tooth might be cracked…or altogether gone."

"My sister is in love with an absolute machine of a man," Albin marveled as the townspeople began standing to their feet.

"Regardless, there's no time to unpack all of that right now," Aleksander changed the subject. "I'm here to save all of you." Sighs of relief and thanks to God were sounded among the townsfolk, but Aleksander began shushing them.

"The remaining soldiers in Zaginiony probably heard the excessive shooting and could be out here any second to investigate. I have a plan to get people out of here. It won't be easy, but we're making for the Romanian border."

"Romanian border?" One woman shrieked. "That's over seven hundred kilometers!"

"We have no other choice," Aleksander told her. "Germany is taking Poland by storm. I've good reason to believe the Soviet Union will start attacking from the east as well. The country is being overrun. It is either that or surrender ourselves to be slaughtered."

That quieted all opposition.

"It's about an eight to ten-day journey," Aleksander announced. "Lord willing, we will make it."

"But not everyone's here," Albin announced.

165

"Aleksander, there are still countless people of Zaginiony being held by the Germans in town! Liliana being one of them!" Aleksander approached Albin and placed a hand on his shoulder.

"I know. I'm going to go save them, too."

"That's suicide," a man in the crowd muttered.

"After what he just did?" Another mentioned.

"They have well over fifty soldiers in town," the first man replied. "And let's be honest, he got lucky with just the few he took out here."

"I have a plan." Aleksander hushed them all again.

The townspeople gathered around Aleksander as the boy took a labored breath.

"About three kilometers south of town, there is a group of six horses tied to a very large English oak tree. It's in a big clearing on the side of the road to Byagoszez. I want all of you to wait there for me for one to two hours. If I or any others from Zaginiony don't show up after that amount of time, I want you all to leave without us. Use the horses for those who have trouble traveling and get yourselves to Romania as fast as you can manage."

"Leave you?" Albin nearly shouted. "We're not going to do that!"

"You have to," Aleksander asserted firmly. "If I or anyone else doesn't show up in an hour, it means I failed and am likely dead. The only people coming for you will be the Germans."

"Why don't we go and fight with you, Aleksander?" One man suggested. "You could use

166

the help."

Several of the townsfolk drew in a nervous breath at that. Fight alongside Aleksander against armed soldiers? The thought was outrageous. Surely, most of them wouldn't last through it.

However, Aleksander calmed their fears by shaking his head.

"I can't allow that," he told the man. "The operation I am about to do is one of stealth rather than a full-frontal assault. I don't want to endanger anyone's life but my own. I also don't want to risk anyone getting caught and being used as a hostage. It's better if I do this myself."

"...You understand that the likelihood of your success is very slim, don't you?" A concerned woman asked the young man.

At that, Aleksander smiled. "My God has done some amazing things with worse odds. I trust He will do so again."

After specific instructions on where to find the horses, the small group of townspeople agreed to wait for Aleksander and the rest of Zaginiony's inhabitants for an hour and a half. Aleksander tried to urge them to only wait an hour, but they persisted that they would give him an hour and a half. Albin was hard to persuade to leave, especially since Liliana was still in town. All the same, Aleksander vowed that he would do everything in his power to rescue her. Albin had to trust that.

With that, they left, and Aleksander was alone. Aleksander began making preparations by checking all of the dead soldiers for more ammunition when he suddenly felt something running down his arm. Glancing at his left shoulder, he suddenly realized that he had been shot. With the adrenaline wearing off, the pain was starting to bleed through. Not only that, but his shirt was started to literally bleed through. His whole left arm ached as the left side of his shirt was slowly being dyed red. Aleksander tried moving his arm. Though he could still move his arm, pain came with each movement. He felt the back of his shoulder and found that there was no exit wound, which meant the bullet was still in his shoulder somewhere. That was both good and bad. Good because Aleksander would only be bleeding from the entry wound of the bullet and would therefore not bleed out as fast. Bad because that meant the more he moved his arm, the more the bullet might create more damage within.

Aleksander took a deep breath, making his signature *"tch"* sound as he snatched a handkerchief from one of the dead *Wehrmacht* soldiers. He put it under his shirt, tying it tightly to his shoulder from under his armpit to try and stop more of the bleeding.

Being shot changed things. It **greatly** changed things. He needed his arm. He needed the strength that both of his arms would provide. Both, not just one. How could he complete this with only one usable arm?

Aleksander then took another breath as he bowed his head. "LORD God of hosts…" He prayed quietly. "You have led me all this way. You have guided my path and made this possible. Please do not abandon me here when I am so close. Give me the strength to deliver this town. Be the mighty sword and the consuming fire I know You to be. In Jesus' holy name, I pray. Amen."

Then, he stood, and as he did, Aleksander felt encouraged and emboldened.

His shoulder didn't hurt. He could move his arm.

CHAPTER SIXTEEN:

The Haunting of Zaginiony

Oberleutnant Hoffmann glanced through the petrified faces of the Zaginiony townspeople as multiple gunshots were going off outside of town. He growled to himself, finding the superfluous gunfire incredibly annoying and unprofessional.

"Sloppy. Wasteful," he thought to himself as he shook his head. *"I'll have to be rather strict with them concerning this after this town is dealt with."*

He had expected a few gunshots to go off all at once, but there were several sporadic shots as well as some shouting that he could pick up. More than likely, the soldiers he had sent hadn't taken their duties as seriously as they ought to have, and some of the Poles had decided to make a run for it.

Regardless, he had a job to do.

"Get everyone else to their homes until the trucks arrive to take them away," he ordered his men. "Any who resist, shoot them. Let's not make this complicated or difficult."

"And her, sir?" One asked, pointing to Hannah. Hannah was standing directly next to Hoffmann. Hoffmann's hand was like a vice grip on the poor girl's shoulder, forbidding her from running.

"Oh, I'll deal with her myself—"

"She's a Hodor." A young man suddenly approached. One of the Zaginiony townspeople.

Hoffmann glared at him. "What?"

"Her name is Hannah Hodor," The young man offered, anxiously fidgeting as he forced a wide smile. "I've had my eyes on her for some time. She's refused to date me over and over again, but I know she'll come around eventually."

Hoffmann was growing rather impatient with this young man. "What is your name?"

"Piotr, sir."

"Piotr," Hoffmann tried out. "Is there some point you have to this hopeless romance tale of yours?"

"Well, seeing as she no longer has a house—" Piotr awkwardly glanced over to the rubble that was once the Hodor estate. "—I was wondering if you might be a friend and allow her to stay with me and my family. Help a guy out?"

Hoffmann stared at Piotr for some time. "Piotr, has anyone told you that you're a terrible liar?"

Piotr did his best to keep his fake smile. "Yes, sir, they have."

"Good to know," Hoffmann declared. "Now, you have three seconds to get out of my sight before I shoot you. One, two…"

Piotr buckled under the pressure. Giving Hannah an apologetic look, he bolted away.

Hannah appreciated that he had tried to save her. She hadn't known Piotr very well, mostly because Liliana wanted nothing to do with him, but at that moment, she regretted that she had not gotten to know him better. As the rest of the townspeople were being herded away to their homes, Hannah was being

171

led away with no one but the *Oberleutnant*.

"So, Miss **Hodor,**" Hoffmann spoke softly as he lit his cigarette. He and Hannah were seated in his car, parked at the edge of the town. His voice, albeit soft, was still incredibly terrifying to Hannah.

She easily perceived the way he emphasized "Hodor," showing that he knew quite well it was fictitious. Hannah had seen this way of dealing with people before. It was a way of talking where everything was heavily implied without directly saying it. It made her panic. She wished he would just be forthright with her. He had already tricked her into revealing her heritage. He had already boasted that he had gotten her. They both knew she was Jewish, and they both knew she was either going to die immediately or be shipped off to a concentration camp.

But just proclaiming her fate was too quick. No, Hoffmann wished for her to suffer psychologically first. True, he certainly didn't have to go through this extra work. He was simply ordered to eliminate all Jews he found holed up in Polish towns as they made their victorious march across the nation. But he took pleasure in drawing it out. He enjoyed fanning the flames of fear in his victim's eyes. He loved watching them break and start confessing and begging before he could even finish the whole speech he had planned.

He couldn't even hold back his grin as he turned to face her. His grin widened as he saw the woman go pale with a horrified stare. Then, Hoffmann paused.

Hoffmann realized that Hannah's look was slightly abnormal. This look of fear was a bit too much. Her eyes were wide, her mouth open in a gasping sort of way, and she was trembling. Hoffmann blinked, wondering if this girl was simply more prone to his tactics. But he then realized that the girl wasn't looking at him. No, she was looking *past* him, outside his car window. To confirm this, she raised a shaking hand and pointed.

Hoffmann turned to see what she was looking at. He responded with an alarmed gasp.

There was a face in his window, staring directly into the car. The eyes looked like they were set on fire, possibly belonging to the devil himself. Before Hoffmann could do anything, a hand smashed through the car window and seized him by the throat. He was quickly being choked, feeling his windpipe being crushed as he was dragged through the window and out of the car.

A horror-struck scream could be heard throughout all of Zaginiony. Several soldiers came running immediately. Hannah was outside of the car, crying and shaking profusely. On the other end of the vehicle was *Oberleutnant* Hoffmann. He lay face-first in the dirt. A soldier by the name of Fischer rolled him over to find his eyes still open. His face was paralyzed in that of shock and fright.

More importantly, the man was dead. Still warm, but unresponsive and not breathing. His throat looked like it was a squished paper cup. Glancing over at the thin, young girl, the soldiers knew this was not her doing. Another soldier inspected the car, seeing the window completely shattered.

"What happened?" Fischer asked the poor girl on the other side of the car. Fischer tried to keep his voice level and sure. He failed. His voice cracked, betraying everyone to know how spooked he was.

No one judged him. They were spooked, too.

Unlike Hoffmann, Fischer could not speak Polish. He had spoken in German, hoping the girl would understand.

Unbeknownst to him, Hannah *could* understand him perfectly. However, she was in such a state of fright that she could not speak. She only muttered and spat out gibberish, still crying out of the terror she had experienced.

Her display made many of the soldiers even more nervous. "She saw something," one of the soldiers gulped.

"An animal?" Another asked his fellows.

"What kind of animal could do this?" Fischer asked, gesturing to their leader with a crushed throat.

No one answered. Instead, they began readying their weapons.

"Who is next in charge?" One of the soldiers questioned. They needed to report this and receive orders as to what should be done.

"*Leutnant* Becker," another told him. "Find him and tell him what we found."

A soldier by the name of Schäfer nodded and began heading into town.

"What about the girl?" Fischer asked as he glanced back at Hannah.

Then, Fischer gasped. The girl was gone.

"She's run off!" He spouted, glancing all around. The other soldiers, now alerted, began searching around as well. Hoffmann's car was on the outskirts of the small town. There were plenty of trees and brush in the surrounding area.

"Leave her," one of the soldiers dismissed, hoping that whatever killed Hoffmann might follow her. "We need to—"

"Gaack!" A terrible gagging sound came from inside the town.

The soldiers all instinctively lifted their rifles, pointing them in the direction of the sound.

No other sound came. All was still.

They all began looking one to another. Without speaking, they all began carefully moving into the town where the sound had come from. They all stepped as lightly and quietly as possible, as if doing so would keep them invisible. Turning onto the main road that ran through town, the soldiers found quite a commotion. Most of the *Wehrmacht* platoon was centered around the church, the tallest building still standing in the little town. At the sight of the rest of their fellows, the small group of soldiers relaxed somewhat. They jogged over to join their comrades, looking to find *Leutnant* Becker to report Hoffmann's demise. But as they approached, they realized their fellows looked just as frightened as they had been.

175

Then, they saw.

Schäfer was hanging from the church steeple. His own belt was wrapped around his throat like a noose and tied to the steeple. Not only that, but his uniform was smeared with blood.

There were small mumblings throughout the group of *Wehrmacht* soldiers.

"How did he get up there like that...?" One muttered to his fellow.

"One of the Poles?" One guessed. "Or a group of them?"

"Impossible." Another shook his head. "Which ones? We were just shoving them back into their homes."

"Enough," Becker himself spoke over them, looking paler than usual himself. "It's clearly just a rogue Pole that we missed. I want him found now. And someone go fetch *Oberleutnant* Hoffmann. He needs to see this."

"*Oberleutnant* Hoffmann is dead." Fischer squeaked.

All eyes turned to them. A palpable silence overcame all of them.

Becker swallowed slowly. "What?"

"Hoffmann was killed by something." Fischer continued explaining. He abandoned all hope of appearing confident and unafraid. He was very frightened, and everyone knew it.

It became quite contagious rather quickly.

"Hoffmann was interrogating that girl." Fischer continued, his voice wavering slightly. "We found his car window shattered, with Hoffmann dead outside his car. His throat was smashed. The girl was too scared to even speak to us. And—" Fischer weighed whether or not he should keep going.

"Yes?" Becker questioned.

"Then she completely vanished," Fischer told him. "Without a sound."

"She likely ran off," One of the other soldiers who had been at the car excused. "But…it's true, we didn't hear her go."

The silence that had permeated the town just moments ago was broken by the sudden fearful chatter between the soldiers.

"This town is cursed."

"There's some sort of creature about. We need to get out of here."

"Schäfer did some terrible things to a few of the girls back in Danzig. Perhaps he had a wraith following him."

"Silence, all of you!" Becker suddenly shouted over his troops. "This is all nonsense! There is no curse or wraith!" But at his yell, there was suddenly a shrieking that came from a nearby barn. Everyone turned to see a cloud of dust that was getting kicked up with a sudden surge of noise.

An entire stampede of horses was suddenly rampaging towards the main road. They looked just as frightened as the *Wehrmacht* soldiers.

And they were coming straight for them.

The soldiers frantically scrambled to get out of the way, but there was only so much room for over forty soldiers to move in such a short amount of time. Gunshots and screams were heard as many Germans were trampled by the horses' charge.

When the animals fled outside of Zaginiony and the dust cleared, various soldiers were found dead. Whether by the stampede or accidental friendly fire. Subordinates, comrades, friends…suddenly gone. The death count was rising very quickly among their ranks, and none of them by any members of the Polish military. Each death was done in a way that felt…unholy. The already spooked soldiers were borderline hysterical at this point. Something otherworldly was going on. They turned to the *leutnant*, who was standing close to the church building. For some odd reason, he was turned to face the door of the church.

"*Leutnant*," Fischer called to Becker, approaching him as many other soldiers did. "Please, let's be done with this town. I say we burn it and leave—"

But Fischer was interrupted when Becker turned to face him. *Leutnant* Becker's throat was slashed. Bleeding out profusely, the man reached out towards Fischer, desperation aflame in his eyes.

This caused Fischer to leap back, screaming. Many other *Wehrmacht* soldiers followed suit, some even looking at the church building itself in horror as if the structure had done it.

Becker collapsed on the ground, blood pooling under him. He died within minutes.

That had done it. Fischer was not about to condemn himself to a gruesome and horrible death by some evil spirit. He didn't even know who the next in charge was, but he was not waiting around to find out.

"There is a demon here!" He shouted to the others, walking away from the church. "I am leaving! If anyone is wise, they'll—"

As Fischer turned away from the church building, he spotted a lone figure standing in the road ahead of him.

Fischer paused, fear gripping him again. But he stopped himself before the panic started setting in. It looked like just a young man. It could have been one of the Poles that they had forced into their homes, coming out to see what all the yelling was about.

However, Fischer's mind was quickly changed when he spotted the great amount of blood that covered the figure. Blood covering his legs. Blood leaking from his hand. Blood smeared all over his shirt.

Then, just as Fischer was trying to find a reasonable explanation for all of it, the young man, ever so slowly, tilted his head to the left. It was done eerily so, partnered with a stare that could startle the bravest of men.

And Fischer was not the bravest of men.

"Evil spirit!" He pointed, his voice breaking once again. The other German soldiers turned and shouted similarly, believing the small figure to be exactly that.

But it wasn't until the ghost smiled that they were all overwhelmed by their fear. The ghost's lips curled

179

back to reveal a smile so wide and haunting that none of those men would ever forget it. It was like its lips had cracked apart to a gleeful, toothy grin that was much too happy to see them.

To top it all, blood began dripping out of its mouth onto the dirt path.

Several soldiers broke at that, dropping all that they were carrying and immediately running. Some, however, did their best to be brave and point their weapons at the ghost. Until it unleashed a blood-curdling roar, like the fabled poltergeist they had heard of in their childhood. As it roared, it very quickly began charging at them. A cacophony of screams echoed out from the *Wehrmacht* soldiers as nearly all of them ran in terror. Those who stayed behind opened fire on the spirit, but it kept advancing upon them without hindrance. It was able to reach the first soldier and slew him easily. That had finally done it for the rest. Convinced they were dealing with a demonic ghost, they dropped their weapons and fled anywhere they could.

One Polish ghost had defeated an entire platoon of *Wehrmacht* soldiers.

CHAPTER SEVENTEEN:
A Scheme Unfolded

Aleksander couldn't help but laugh. Not a taunting, mocking laugh, but a laugh of sheer relief. His plan had worked perfectly. Absolutely everything had worked out, and the greatest threat to the people of Zaginiony was fleeing for their lives from what they believed was a vengeful spirit.

In truth, it was him.

Aleksander had been the one to crush Hoffmann's throat after dragging him through his own car window. That was admittedly not planned on Aleksander's part. Since Hannah and Liliana truly did look so alike, Aleksander had believed that the *Oberleutnant* had taken his beloved prisoner. At that thought, Aleksander had been overcome with rage. He allowed his anger to take ahold of him and acted rashly. Though he had quickly disposed of Hoffmann, Aleksander had hurt his right hand. His knuckles were bleeding due to punching through the glass of the car. Several large cuts had been carved into his arm as well because of the broken glass. But what was done was done, and it was only after killing Hoffmann that Aleksander had perceived that the shrieking girl was not Liliana. Hearing other soldiers approaching, he hid himself.

Aleksander had been the one to steal Hannah away from the Germans. Fearing that they might just shoot her, Aleksander clamped a hand over her mouth before rapidly dragging the terrified girl away out of sight while the soldiers were preoccupied with their fallen commanding officer. Aleksander had little time to explain to Hannah what he was doing, so he simply ordered her to stay hidden and that he was there to help.

Aleksander had been the one to take down Schäfer and hang him from the church steeple. Feeling it was rather sacrilegious, Aleksander prayed that God would not hold it against him to sully the church building with a dead *Wehrmacht* soldier. Schäfer had barely made it to the main road before a knife was lodged in the base of his neck. He died nearly instantly, albeit making a great deal of noise.

Aleksander acted quickly to rush the body behind the church building as the rest of the *Wehrmacht* soldiers were returning from forcibly putting the Zaginiony townsfolk back into their homes. They had heard the noise as well, but seemed to be looking around aimlessly, unsure of where it had come from, and thank the Lord, Aleksander had found that many people did not look up. Aleksander scaled the back wall of the church, clutching Schäfer's corpse with one arm. This was the most difficult part of the entire operation. He was climbing the church building with over twice the weight he was used to and having to work with only one arm. The other arm, which was clinging tightly to a dead man's body, had also been shot and was still bleeding. But Aleksander had believed this part of the ruse was the most crucial. If

182

he were to survive the night and save everyone in Zaginiony, he needed to scare off the Germans. And Schäfer's body would be the first spark to a wildfire of fear.

Reaching the roof of the church, Aleksander had found that Schäfer's neck wound had bled out all over his uniform, giving it a nice, terrifying touch. Aleksander removed Schäfer's belt and tied it expertly around the steeple as well as Schäfer's neck and pushed him out to hang before his Nazi audience. By the time someone had finally noticed the body hanging from the steeple, Aleksander was already back down on the ground and heading to the next part of his plan.

Aleksander had not only been the one to unleash Kowalski's barn full of horses but ensured that they ran like their lives depended on it. Aleksander had worked with some of Kowalski's horses before leaving Poland. Kowalski had one particular horse that was named Crazy. Rightly so, for she had a very wild temperament. She loved to kick people, Aleksander himself being one of her previous victims. Sneaking into the barn, snatching a piece of leather, and whipping Crazy in the rear was all he had to do. Crazy began thrashing about and violently kicking in every direction. Thankfully, her behavior became contagious to all of the other horses.

Aleksander opened the barn door wide, and they began racing out frantically. With all of the horses sufficiently frightened and bolting out of the barn, Aleksander was able to leap on one as it rode off.

Pressing himself down as far as he could, he prayed that he wouldn't be seen among the animals.

And he wasn't.

This entire part of his plan was not only to frighten the general soldiers more, but to eliminate leadership.

Aleksander knew just by Hoffmann's uniform that he was the man in charge. After retreating off the church roof, Aleksander had pinpointed the next man in charge: Becker. Everyone was turning to him for answers and orders. To further drive the terror into the soldiers' hearts, he needed to be taken out.

And he was. Aleksander rode close in the chaos of the stampede and was able to slice his throat with his knife. No one saw him do it, and the effect worked perfectly. The German soldiers were shaking. They just needed one final push.

Aleksander had been the "ghost" standing in the middle of the road. Jumping off his panicked horse, Aleksander hid until the animals were gone, and the soldiers had discovered Becker dead. As he waited for the right moment to move out into the open, Aleksander was forced to spit out more blood. At this point, he had found that his tooth had been knocked out entirely and was forced to spit it out of his mouth. With that, a rush of blood was flooding his mouth due to the dislodged tooth. Aleksander figured he could take advantage of that, as well as the blood that still dripped from his left shoulder and right arm, he began smearing the blood all over himself in order to encourage the right reaction from the *Wehrmacht* soldiers. Stepping out into the middle of the main road and smiling his largest, most unhinged smile at the soldiers did just the thing. The blood leaking from his mouth due to his tooth injury was an exemplary topping to this guise he had placed.

But something occurred that Aleksander had hoped against. Rightly being called the "fight or flight reflex," the soldiers who didn't start running began raising their guns at him. Were they scared? Absolutely, but that didn't mean they wouldn't try shooting this perceived ghost. So, Aleksander switched from the crazed, gleeful spirit to the monstrous, wrathful killer. Pushing more of the soldiers to run, his tactic was working as he charged at them, screaming as loud as he could. But a few shot at him before he was able to reach his first victim. After snapping the soldier's neck blindingly fast, it seemed that the rest of the soldiers ran without thinking of stopping to take on a ghost.

Aleksander's plan had worked. For that, he repeatedly began bowing his head and thanking the Lord over and over. But something didn't feel right. His shoulder began aching terribly again, but also his... Leg.

Looking down, Aleksander groaned at seeing a fresh bullet wound in his right leg. He had been shot again. One of the soldiers, when firing during his desperate charge, had hit him. He had not even had time to treat the first bullet wound, and the one in his leg felt far worse. Far more painful.

Aleksander did what he could to apply a

tourniquet to his leg, but he was unable to stand on it again. Furthermore, he was beginning to feel dizzy and nauseous. If he had been able to think clearly, he would have realized that he had lost a fair amount of blood, gone through a physically exhausting mission of rescuing his town, and been running on nothing but adrenaline the entire time.

His body was out of resources, and he needed medical attention as well as rest.

But Aleksander wasn't able to think clearly. So, instead, he simply passed out on the road.

CHAPTER EIGHTEEN:
Racing Against the Night

Liliana knew something was wrong…or, perhaps, something was *right* when she heard the frantic screams of the *Wehrmacht* soldiers. Peering through the door of the house she was shoved into, she found that Zaginiony was empty.

She blinked twice. Surely they didn't just… leave? She shook her head, opening the door a little more. If they were going to just leave, what was all the screaming about?

Slowly poking her head out of the open door, she glanced all around the town. Not a German in sight.

Feeling slightly more confident, she opened the door fully and walked out of the house. She saw others were doing so out of the small houses they had been placed in.

Then, she spotted a German soldier hanging from the church steeple.

"What happened?" She whispered to herself in frightful awe. Inspecting the church more closely, she found several *Wehrmacht* soldier bodies lying lifeless near it. Her gaze followed the trail of bodies until she spotted Hannah on the road, kneeling over one of the bodies.

"Hannah!" Liliana called. She was so relieved to see her dear friend still alive. She began running to her when the thought occurred to her…

*"Oh, my word, did **Hannah** do this?"* Liliana

wondered. But as she drew closer, she realized that the body Hannah was standing over was different from the German soldiers. It was just a simple, small, ordinary man.

Then, a terrible gasp erupted from her. It was Aleksander.

"What happened?!" Liliana screamed at Hannah.

"He's alive!" Hannah told Liliana with a worried expression. "He saved my life—no, *all* of our lives! We need to help him!"

"What happened?!" Liliana screamed again at Hannah.

"I don't know!" Hannah screamed back at Liliana. "But instead of yelling at me, go find a doctor or something! He's dying!"

Liliana turned around to the other Zaginiony inhabitants who were still carefully exiting their homes.

"HELP!!!" Liliana screamed with all of her might. "We need a doctor! Does anyone know how to help him?!" Unbeknownst to her, Liliana's scream "help" could actually be heard by the still-fleeing Germans. It made them run all the faster, believing that the ghost was now attacking the inhabitants of Zaginiony.

Zaginiony had one doctor. Liliana hadn't noticed, but when Albin had made his outburst against Hoffmann, the doctor was rallied up with those who were going to be shot out in the forest. Being saved by Aleksander, the doctor was perfectly fine, albeit far from Zaginiony and unable to help save

Aleksander's life.

However, since the doctor had been getting on in years, he was hoping to pass on his knowledge to someone who might one day replace him. He knew that medical school was terribly expensive. Only one family could afford it, that being the Hodors. However, both Liliana and Albin seemed to have no interest in that field of work. So, taking on an apprentice for a very small fee, the Zaginiony doctor took one young man under his wing to apprentice him in a field of work the young man considered would be a great occupation to attract Liliana's attention.

That young man was Piotr.

"I can help." Piotr came running after snagging some supplies from the doctor's practice.

"Piotr?" Liliana couldn't contain her amazement. "Since when do *you* know anything about being a doctor?"

"You would know if you paid any attention to me at all," Piotr grumbled with some slight bitterness. "Hold on… Aleksander?"

Before Piotr could say anything further, Liliana seized him by the shoulders and gave him a very frightening glare.

"If you refuse to save him simply because of all those fights you two used to have, I swear, I will—I will—I don't know what I'll do yet, but it will be *terrible!* Please save him!"

"Relax, relax." Piotr brushed her off him. "I'm not *that* petty."

189

He quickly began examining Aleksander.

"From what I can tell, his biggest problem is blood loss," Piotr mused. "If he loses over 40%, he'll likely die."

"How much has he lost?"

"I don't know."

"You don't know?!"

"No, I don't know!" Piotr fumed at her. "I wasn't carefully watching this imbecile and recording every drop of blood! Be patient with me in this!"

"We don't have time to be patient!" Liliana raged back at him.

"Liliana," Hannah took hold of her arm. Both Liliana and Piotr looked at Hannah.

"I'm sorry, but you're only making this worse," Hannah told her. "Let Piotr do what he can to save Aleksander."

Liliana begrudgingly nodded. "Okay. I'm sorry."

With that, Piotr began to work.

Albin had lately picked up a nasty habit of not being the most obedient when everyone stressed he should be. The hour and a half was about to pass, and he could not bear to leave behind both his sister and Aleksander to die at the hands of the Germans. A few individuals volunteered to go back to Zaginiony with him to see if Aleksander had been successful or not. Expecting the worst, they sneaked to the edge of Zaginiony. However, to Albin's delight, he found no one in town save the townsfolk of Zaginiony that he knew.

Not a German in sight.

"God sent us a mighty man indeed," Albin marveled as they began running into the town. No sooner had he said it did he spot Liliana.

"Liliana!" He called, racing to her.

"Albin!" She gasped in delight, running to her brother. The siblings shared a tearful embrace as both rejoiced to see the other still alive.

"Oh, I thought you had been killed!" Liliana wailed as she held her brother tight.

"I worried the same for you when Aleksander came back here alone."

"Aleksander saved you?" Liliana broke away from the hug.

"Of course." Albin nodded to her. "Surely, you must have seen him. What else would drive the Germans off?"

"Oh, I've seen him…" Liliana turned a worried look back to where Piotr was working on Aleksander.

Albin followed his sister's gaze to see Zaginiony's savior lying in the dirt.

"No!" Albin cried. "He's been killed?"

"No, but he has been shot," Liliana explained solemnly. "Piotr is doing what he can."

As if on cue, Piotr glanced up from working on Aleksander and gestured for Liliana to come back.

"So, I have good news and bad news," Piotr explained to Liliana and Albin as he wiped the blood off his hands. "There are two bullets still in

Aleksander. That's both good and bad. The bullets kind of helped clog up the holes, so he didn't bleed out as much. Of course, it's not good that they're still there, and they will probably have to be taken out eventually. But I've stitched up his wounds.

"He's not bleeding out anymore, but I don't know if he's lost too much blood or not. Furthermore, another big issue is infection. That could kill him just as easily as blood loss. I'm—"

"Get to it, Piotr," Albin grunted impatiently.

Piotr could tell that Liliana didn't need all of the explanation, either.

"He needs a real doctor," Piotr told them. "Better yet, a hospital."

"We're at war, Piotr," Liliana interjected fearfully. "What hospital can we get him to? Surely not Danzig's."

"No," Piotr agreed. "But maybe Warsaw's?"

"That's too far." Albin ground his teeth with worry. "How are we going to get him all that way before…?"

Albin didn't want to finish that sentence. Liliana took a deep breath. "I can take him."

"How?"

"By horse."

"That's still a three-day ride, not counting stops and rest periods," Albin mentioned.

"I'll have to make do." Liliana mustered her courage. "Aleksander came all this way to save us. Now I will go as far as I need to in order to save him."

192

Without another word, Liliana rushed off to find any horse that might still be available. Albin rushed to follow after her, unsure if this was the best course of action. Hannah and Piotr were left standing over an unconscious Aleksander.

Hannah glanced over at him. "I…I'm Hannah."

"Hi, Hannah," Piotr replied awkwardly. "I'm Piotr."

"I-I thought you were really brave," Hannah confessed to him. "Trying to help me earlier with Hoffmann. And helping Aleksander."

Piotr blushed. "Thank you. I, uh…I think you're really pretty."

"Oh, thank you," Hannah responded, also blushing.

The two then sat in a horribly uncomfortable silence until Liliana and Albin returned.

"Liliana!" Albin pestered his sister.

"Not now, Albin!" Liliana cut him off as she searched through Kowalski's barn. She hadn't realized that Aleksander had released all of the horses. The entire barn was empty, causing Liliana to tense up with anxiety and worry.

"But Liliana, you—!"

Liliana, at boiling point, spun around to face her brother. "Albin, stop! You are my brother, and I love you, but I need to figure out how I'm going to keep Aleksander alive, okay?!"

Liliana instantly choked up after that, having heard herself admit that Aleksander could die. She couldn't face that reality. Not when they had come so far, and Aleksander had done so much to save them all!

But Liliana wasn't going to just break down and cry. She had to find some answer. She had to save her beloved! She had to—!

Albin suddenly cut her from her thoughts. He did this simply by holding up a set of keys.

Liliana blinked at them.

"Hoffmann's car," Albin stated quietly. "Much faster than a horse."

Liliana embraced her brother, kissing his forehead. "You are a miracle, Albin!"

"Good for you to finally admit it," Albin laughed as he handed her the keys.

Liliana took no more time. She raced back out to Piotr and Hannah.

"We have a plan," she told both of them as Albin caught up to her. "Hannah, you go with the rest of the people to find where Albin's group is waiting." Hannah nodded before joining up with the others. The rest of the town seemed to be gathering some quick supplies together before moving out with the rest of the group that Albin had originally come with.

"Why just her?" Piotr pointed at Hannah as she began heading off.

"Because you're coming with us." Liliana gestured to herself, Aleksander, and Albin.

"On a horse?"

"In Hoffmann's car."

"The Nazi's car?" Piotr started looking rather

worried. "That sounds an awful lot like a bad idea. What if we're stopped by more German soldiers?"

"That's why we need you."

"What?!" Piotr squeaked.

Liliana and Albin ignored Piotr's outcry as they both began to gently lift Aleksander together. They began carrying him over to Hoffmann's car. Piotr quickly followed alongside.

"Please tell me what could possibly be going through those minds to think that I would be helpful in a situation like that!" Piotr expressed helplessly.

"Piotr, get the door," Liliana ordered him as they got Aleksander next to the car door. Piotr obeyed and opened the rear left door, and Albin and Liliana gently laid him down on the seat.

"Get Hoffmann's uniform," Liliana told Albin. "Then go get a soldier's uniform from one of the dead Germans. One that will fit you."

Albin nodded before getting to work. Liliana then turned to Piotr.

"There are several reasons why we need you. First, you can monitor Aleksander with a better understanding than either Albin or I can. You can let us know how well or unwell he's doing. Secondly, you're old enough."

"Old enough for what?" Piotr was getting an ill feeling in the pit of his stomach.

"Here." Albin suddenly popped up next to him, pushing Hoffmann's officer uniform into his hands

"Absolutely not!" Piotr objected, noting that Hoffmann's body was now only in his undergarments. "I am not posing as a German officer!"

195

"We need you to." Liliana pressed as Albin ran off to get himself a uniform. "It won't work any other way. You look old enough to be Hoffmann. Albin's too young. Could he pose as an average soldier? Sure, but there's no way, if we were to be stopped by Germans, that he could fool anyone into thinking he was old enough to be an officer. I obviously can't do it, either."

"But I can't speak German!"

"Albin can."

"He can?"

"Yes, funny story actually." Liliana allowed herself a small, anxious-sounding laugh. "Did it so he could properly understand when I was insulting him in it. Anyway, what's important is that Albin will do all the talking, posing as your driver."

Piotr stood there for a moment. "And why should I do this at all? I've already risked my neck enough this night."

Liliana's eyes lit up with anger. She pointed at Aleksander, lying in the car. "And thanks to him, nearly everyone in this town, including you, will have the chance to keep living. He didn't have to come back for us."

Piotr scoffed. "He didn't come back for 'us,' he came back for you. The rest of us are just reaping the benefits."

Albin suddenly came back, dressed as a *Wehrmacht* soldier. He even had a rifle slung over his shoulder.

"Ready," he told both of them.

"Well, Piotr?" Liliana asked Piotr pointedly.

Piotr sighed.

Each individual's role was clear. Albin was the driver. Piotr was posing as Hoffmann, sitting in the back. Next to him were Aleksander and Liliana, both still in their normal clothes. They would both be considered prisoners, posing as themselves. The reason? They held vital information that "Hoffmann" needed to get out of them. With all of that understood, Albin sped off at breakneck speed.

"I've always wanted to try this!" He yelled from the front. "If Aleksander's life weren't on the line, I would have so much more fun with this!"

"He's driven a car before, right?" Piotr asked Liliana with no little amount of worry.

Albin came up to a relatively sharp turn and took it so fast that the car almost lost control. That, in turn, answered Piotr's question.

"Liliana, why is he driving?!"

"I *told* you!" Liliana answered back. "This is our best option!"

Albin took another sharp turn, resulting in Piotr, Liliana, and an unconscious Aleksander all flopping to the right side of the back seat.

"Albin!" Liliana screamed at him. "For goodness' sake, drive with a little more sanity! This whole ruse of you being a driver will be found out the second any German soldier sees us!"

"And that's only if you don't kill us back here!"
Piotr added.

Albin did ease up but still kept a pretty fast speed. Aleksander needed a hospital, and Warsaw was around 318 kilometers from Zaginiony. Since they were in a car instead of riding on horseback, the trip would be much faster. Instead of being a three-day journey, it would be closer to a three-hour drive. Infinitely better, but time was most definitely of the essence. For most of the trip, the young individuals drove along without any issues. After all, it was the dead of night. Liliana constantly asked Albin if he was doing well enough, sleep-wise. Albin repeatedly told her that he was fine and would be fine. Piotr occasionally checked to see how Aleksander was holding up. A few took turns sleeping, and Liliana prayed often.

She began praying harder when they saw a makeshift check in the middle of the road. Three German soldiers stood next to the road. One of them walked out, lifting his hand up in a "stop" position as the vehicle drew near.

"Oh, no," Piotr whimpered. "I hope they don't ask me any questions. We're sunk if they do!"

"Calm down," Liliana hissed at him. "They won't ask you any questions. Just look the part."

"I should pretend I'm sleeping!" Piotr smiled at the idea. "They wouldn't wake a sleeping officer!"

"Sleeping? With two unbound prisoners in the back with you?" Liliana flared up at him. "Real smart! Just act like a pompous German officer. Point

198

your pistol at us."

"Point my pistol—? No! What if I accidentally shoot?"

"'Accidentally shoot'? Just don't pull the trigger!" Liliana gave him the most furious glare. "What are you, five? Be a man, Piotr!"

"I can't believe I had eyes for you," Piotr muttered under his breath as he gingerly pointed the pistol at Liliana and Aleksander.

The three Poles quieted down as they pulled up to the three Germans.

"I can't believe we're stuck out here at this unholy hour," Claus groaned.

"Better than being on the front lines if you ask me," Dieter told his comrade, stretching out his arms. "All we have to do is find anything suspicious. Make sure people aren't crossing who ought not be. So simple!"

"And boring!" Claus groaned again. "I want some action!"

"You'll get it, Claus." The older Werner quieted him. "But I'm with Dieter. Don't be too eager for the violence. When it arrives, you may rescind your desire for it."

The three soldiers stopped talking when they noticed a vehicle approaching. By the look of it, a German officer's vehicle. The three soldiers all gave each other a worried glance. Claus made sure he looked professional as he stepped out on the road and put up his hand in a "stop" motion. The window was already down, and the driver gave an awkward smile.

"Evening," he said.

Claus got an off feeling from him. He couldn't quite place it, but something didn't feel right. He took a moment to look in the back seat. He saw an officer. An *Oberleutnant*, by the look of him. He was pointing a gun at the head of a young civilian girl.

"Evening, *soldat*..." Claus said eventually, as he peered back at the driver. He waited expectantly for the driver's name.

The driver froze for a moment, looking like he was having trouble swallowing.

"Schmidt," he suddenly barked, forcing a smile.

"Schmidt," Claus repeated. "Papers, please."

"The *Oberteutant* has some urgent business with the commanding officer at the front." Schmidt shook his head, suddenly getting a rather sour look.

Claus blinked. "I'm sorry, what? '*Oberteutant*'?" In that moment, Schmidt's face was washed over with fear at his clear mistake. Claus even caught the girl in the back wince.

"*Oberleutant*." Schmidt quickly corrected, letting out an exaggerated laugh. "Forgive me, it's been a long night. We've come all the way from Zaginiony."

Claus didn't reply. This was looking more and more suspicious. Claus took a moment to glance back at Dieter and Werner, but both were hardly paying attention.

"*Fools.*" He thought to himself in irritation. "*I suppose this is all up to me. Naturally.*"

"Aren't you a little young to be a driver to an officer?" Claus approached the vehicle, making sure his rifle was ready.

Schmidt pursed his lips. "I'm a very good driver."

"Are you now?" Claus tightened the grip on his rifle. "I think we might need to take a closer look—" But he was suddenly interrupted by several gunshots erupting from the back of the car.

Piotr couldn't handle the pressure anymore. He knew nothing of what Albin and the soldier were talking about, but he was certainly no idiot. He saw how the soldier narrowed his eyes suspiciously at Albin. He noticed how Liliana winced when Albin apparently misspoke.

He was pretty sure they were already caught. So, whipping the pistol away from Liliana's head, he began firing through the back window. His aim was terrible, missing every single soldier even after firing all of the bullets in the gun. But it was enough to make all of them dive to the ground.

"What are you doing?!" Both Liliana and Albin shouted at Piotr.

"Saving our rear ends! Now drive, drive, drive!" Piotr screamed.

Albin slammed his foot on the accelerator, causing the tires to squeal as they peeled out past the checkpoint. Several rifle shots were heard from the three soldiers, most of them hitting the speeding vehicle. However, as they drove out of sight, each person began checking themselves to see if they had been hit.

"Were you hit?" Piotr asked Liliana.

"No, I'm fine. You?" Liliana replied. Then, she called up to her brother. "Albin, did you get shot?"

"I'm pretty certain no," Albin answered, patting himself down with one arm as he steered with the other.

Piotr checked Aleksander. "Aleksander's uninjured, too."

He paused.

"Well, maybe 'uninjured' isn't the right word," he corrected. "There are at least no *new* bullet holes in him."

CHAPTER NINETEEN:

A Promise Kept

Aleksander opened his eyes, unsure of where he was. He felt himself in a bed, though not the comfiest one he had ever been in. A slight breeze came from an open window behind him. He felt absolutely awful, his head having a terrible throb. He also felt resounding aches, emanating from his left arm and leg as well.

"What...?" He thought to himself, trying to remember what had happened. "Where am I?"

Suddenly, it all started coming back to him. Zaginiony. Scaring off the soldiers. Getting shot.

Now more aware, he started glancing all around him, finding himself to be in a hospital room full of other patients. Many of them were wounded, soldier and civilian alike.

Aleksander sat up slowly, trying to force himself to remember how he got there. He remembered clearing the Germans out of Zaginiony. He remembered putting on the tourniquet. Then...it was a blank from there.

"Aleksander?" Her voice suddenly caused all the worry and agitation to cease.

He turned to see her in the doorway, her face beaming. She was shining like an angelic being as the sun reflected off her face.

His Liliana.

"Liliana…" He barely whispered.

Before he knew it, she was at his bedside, wrapping her arms around him. He instantly did likewise, pulling her close and thanking God that he was able to see her again. Safe and happy.

It had been a very difficult four years, but they had made it back to each other.

Aleksander took this embrace to reignite every sensory feeling he could concerning Liliana. The soft warmth of her touch. The lovely scent of her hair. The gentle rhythm of her breathing. But he suddenly stopped when he felt a bandage on her arm. He pulled away from their hug to look at it.

"Were you hurt?" He asked her softly, caressing the bandage gently.

Liliana only laughed in response. "Yes and no."

Aleksander gazed at her with some confusion.

"Weren't you curious why you have one?" She pointed to his right arm.

Looking over, Aleksander saw he had an identical bandage covering the crease of his arm. He put the pieces together as he looked back at Liliana.

"I needed a blood transfusion," he concluded.

"And I was happy to be your donor." Liliana smiled lovingly. "Good news; we're compatible."

She then placed her hands in his, a somber look overcoming her. "You had done so much for us, coming back and saving everyone. I wanted to do everything I could to save you."

"Where are we?"

"Warsaw."

"How did you get me here?"

"We borrowed a car." Liliana smiled a little nervously. "The owner…wasn't using it at the time. Thank the Lord, we made it."

Aleksander, overwhelmed with emotion, pulled Liliana in for another hug. There, they held each other.

They held each other so long that it made others in the room uncomfortable, but even after their embrace ended, it didn't feel like enough for them.

Aleksander was urged more time to recover, but time was not something they had. September 15th came, and Warsaw was now a rather dangerous place to be. The Battle of the Bzura was taking place not too far off. Aleksander's time for recovery had allowed the rest of Zaginiony to catch up to their current location. With everyone meeting up to praise and honor their hero, it was a rather special moment for Aleksander. All the same, he gave the glory to God, for he knew that he never could have come from New York to Poland, single-handedly rout an entire platoon of German soldiers, and save his town all in just ten days in his own power.

It was a miracle, and no one denied that. That being said, Aleksander still believed their retreat to the south was still vital. Reports were coming in that the German forces were pushing back the Polish military. There was talk of a retreat to the Romanian Bridgehead. And so, the inhabitants of

Zaginiony began making their way to Romania just as they planned.

Traveling along, Aleksander was forced to be near the back of the pack. He had been offered a horse by nearly everyone, but denied the need for one, much like his father would have. Instead, he was more than delighted to walk next to the woman of his dreams, finally being reunited with her. And even though they were racing against time and the vicious machines of Hitler's war, Aleksander couldn't shake the euphoric feeling he had of finally being back with the woman who held his heart.

"Thank you for keeping your promise," Liliana whispered to Aleksander as he hobbled along the road.

"I was serious about it when I told you I would come back." Aleksander couldn't help but smile. "Did you doubt?"

"Yes," Liliana confessed. "Would you forgive me for that?"

"Nothing to forgive." Aleksander beamed at her. "Though…there are a few things that still need to be done. Stop walking for a moment."

"What? Why?"

"Humor me."

So, Liliana stopped walking. Aleksander stood right next to her and, in one fluid swoop, Aleksander swept her off her feet and began carrying her.

"Aleksander Kurtz!" Liliana screeched. "What are you doing?"

"I have to fulfill all of my covenant." He was grinning from ear to ear as he walked along the road with Liliana in his arms. "Part of that was taking you up in my arms."

"Goodness, you're still injured!" Liliana scolded. "You shouldn't be carrying me after just recovering from being shot!"

"Just for a bit longer," Aleksander told her. "By the way, there's one other thing in the covenant we haven't addressed."

"What's that?"

"Will you marry me?" Aleksander asked her.

Liliana gave a small gasp. "What took you so long to ask me that? Of course!"

EPILOGUE:

A Ghost Story

Oberleutnant Richter marched through the supposedly "haunted" town of Zaginiony as a few cowering soldiers followed behind him. Richter had already been told numerous stories from Hoffmann's platoon of a haunting spirit, "the Polish Ghost," they were calling it. Evidently, this creature had slain two officers as well as multiple soldiers single-handedly.

Seeing the aftermath for himself, Richter was tempted to be a believer at first glance. But upon further inspection of the evidence, he saw telltale signs that this was no ghost. His first indication of this was when he walked among the bodies of the soldiers outside the town. The ones who had taken Albin and the others to shoot them. Among them, Richter found a lone pistol that was not of German make. Furthermore, he found that several fallen soldiers were killed by gunfire.

"Why would a ghost need a gun?" Richter mused to himself.

Now, moving through the rest of the town, he could see simple explanations for everything. However, whoever this man was, he was not someone to trifle with. His physical strength was superior to anyone Richter had ever known. Hoffmann was a perfect example of that. Still lying at the very edge of town with a collapsed throat. The force it would have taken to crush Hoffmann's throat had to be outstanding.

The only thing that was still a bit of a puzzle was the corpse of Schäfer, hanging from the church steeple. In the daylight, it was easy to see that he had a puncture wound at the base of his neck, likely from a knife. The soldiers' stories of the terrible sound he had made matched with such a wound.

"But how did he get up there?" Richter asked himself.

Richter had already taken note of the belt that was used to tie him to the steeple of the church. Richter decided to walk around the church. The soldiers didn't follow, fearing that the church had been the source of the vengeful spirit. However, as Richter came to the back of the building, he saw bloodstains stretching up the wall and onto the roof.

"He climbed." Richter raised his eyebrows, rather impressed. *"With Schäfer's dead-weight body. Strong indeed. A very capable man was defending this town."*

Richter began nodding to himself, all the evidence now pointing to a particularly strong individual putting on a show for the *Wehrmacht*. No dark magic or haunting wraiths. Just a desperate man trying to protect his own.

Richter couldn't help but smile, feeling a sense of respect for whoever had done this. Because of this "ghost's" actions, an entire town was able to be spared from Hitler's camps.

Richter's smile faded just at that thought. He groaned, shaking his head. He didn't like that man. He didn't like his ideology. But orders were orders, and Germany was, in fact, seeing a great deal of prosperity lately. Anything was better than the depression they had been facing since 1918. Even...bringing misery to others.

"Sometimes you have to take the bad in order to get the good." Richter shrugged to himself, trying to calm his guilty conscience. *"What's better? Other people's suffering or your own people's suffering?"*

For that moment, Richter was able to appease the guilt he felt.

"Oberleutnant!" He heard the call of some soldiers, still at the front of the church. He could tell by their cry that they were beginning to think he had been claimed by the ghost.

Richter allowed himself a quiet chuckle as he began heading towards the front of the church. The soldiers who waited for him gave sighs of relief, confirming Richter's suspicions.

"Did you find anything?" One questioned.

Richter glanced back at the church. "No. Truly confounding, this whole situation. I can't explain it."

The soldiers began nodding, feeling that their terror was validated. They all began talking at once about how other soldiers didn't believe them, how there was clearly no other explanation, etc.

But Richter wasn't listening. He was wondering if he had made the right call to essentially tell these soldiers that what they had experienced was truly supernatural.

Inwardly, he shrugged to himself. It probably didn't matter. He just didn't want to expose the ruse, after how much effort the "Polish Ghost" had put into it. More so, Richter was still so impressed that it worked so well. He knew he couldn't do it now, but superstitions of the troops would have to be addressed so as to keep this from happening in the future.

"*Oberleutnant…*" One soldier pulled him from his thoughts.

"Hm?" Richter gave him his attention.

"What should we do about this town?" He asked, looking around worriedly.

"Bury our dead." Richter began listing. "Then raze it. There's nothing here of worth to us."

"But the Polish Ghost!" The soldiers began objecting.

"The Polish Ghost defends those he loves." Richter silenced them as he began walking out of the small town. "He is a long way from here."

THE END

Dear Reader,

As you've read through this book, you've probably noticed how much of the story centers around Christianity. Now, I don't know what you particularly feel about Christianity, but I would like to say something, if that's all right. What I am about to tell you does not come from a heart that is holier than-thou or just wanting you to join my church. I tell you this because I am concerned for your soul. It's similar to a man at a beach who sees a shark in the water. Some of those who are swimming in the ocean don't notice the danger. So what should he do? Make them aware of the danger by yelling "SHARK!" And that's what I'm endeavoring to do. I want to warn you of the danger that's coming at the end of your life.

Recently, there have been a decent number of people I have known that suddenly passed away. Most were unexpected and very shocking. It reminded me of a rather depressing truth: death is coming for all of us. We don't know when and we don't know how, but death will eventually come. And, for some, I kept thinking to myself, "Where are they now?" I didn't know some of their faiths or beliefs. But I believe in a God who made the heavens and the earth. I believe that, in the beginning, the world was perfect. I believe that mankind sinned against God, thus shattering the perfection of creation. I believe that all have sinned and are worthy of judgment. I believe that Jesus Christ, God in human flesh, lived a sinless life and died on the cross so He might pay the price of our sin for us. I believe that anyone who calls upon Him will be saved from a literal, eternal hell. And I, as one of His believers, am to go out and tell others of His salvation so that they can be saved as well.

In today's age, there are thousands of faiths that someone can believe in. And people flock to religions because we, as humanity, have an inner knowledge that there is something bigger than all of us that first brought everything into being. Even atheists know that a higher being exists out there. They just choose to reject it. When my friends died, it forced me to think of their eternal destination. Their opportunity to choose is past, and they are either in heaven with the Lord or burning in the penetrating darkness of hell. This is not the most cheery stuff, I admit. But, as I said earlier, I'm concerned for your eternal destination, and I don't want anyone to go to hell. I wouldn't wish that on my worst enemy. So, if you'll permit me, I'd like to tell you about how you can get away from the shark, so to speak. Now, before I get into it, I will let you know that I'm not trying to make you my disciple or anything. I'm not trying to get accolades for converting someone to Christianity, and I'm most certainly not trying to force you to become a Christian against your will. No, I'm telling you about it so you can make the choice for yourself. From my perspective, people are in grave danger. And, again, we don't know when our life will end. So what kind of person would I be if I believed in a real place called hell, but never told anyone how to be rescued from it?

So, without further ado, I'd like to lay out the steps of salvation, if that's all right with you.

1. God is holy and cannot be in the presence of sin.

"For I am the LORD that bringeth you up out of the land of Egypt, to be your God: ye shall therefore be holy, for I am holy."
Leviticus 11:45

"There is none holy as the LORD: for there is none beside Thee: neither is there any rock like our God."
1 Samuel 2:2

"Holy, holy, holy, Lord God Almighty, which was, and is, and is to come."
Revelation 4:8b

Holy is a word that means "set apart," "morally blameless," or "sacred." Essentially, it means to be without sin. Since God is holy, associating with sin would nullify His holiness. It's like mixing oil with water or trying to put light and darkness together. It can't happen. If God and humanity are going to be in each other's presence, one of them needs to change. And it's not going to be God.

2. Every human is a sinner. Even the tiniest sin makes you incapable of being in God's presence and worthy of His wrath.

"For all have sinned, and come short of the glory of God;"
Romans 3:23

This is where some believe that they are "good enough" with God because they haven't committed the big sins like murder, rape, etc., but if you think that, just look at the Ten Commandments and ask yourself, "Have I broken any of these?"

1. Thou shalt have no other gods before Me.
2. Thou shalt not make unto thee any graven image.
3. Thou shalt not take the name of the LORD thy God in vain.
4. Remember the sabbath to keep it holy.
5. Honor thy father and mother.
6. Thou shalt not kill.
7. Thou shalt not commit adultery.
8. Thou shalt not steal.
9. Thou shalt not bear false witness.
10. Thou shalt not covet.

People usually acknowledge that they've broken at least one of the Ten Commandments (usually the one that deals with lying, at least). But, in the New Testament, Jesus added a higher standard to a few of these commandments. He said that if you held anger in your heart towards someone, you've committed murder in your heart. He also said if you look upon someone with lust who is not your spouse, you're committing mental adultery (adultery here is actually referring to sexual sin in general, not necessarily the specific act of cheating on a spouse, though that is included). Now, most people have done those things as well, which makes them lying, murdering adulterers. And that's just three of the Ten Commandments. But even if someone had only broken one little aspect of God's law, the New Testament also says this:

"For whosoever shall keep the whole law, and yet offend in one point, he is guilty of all."
James 2:10

It's like having a string tied to a ball. The string has ten knots in it, representing the Ten Commandments. If someone were to cut the knots with scissors, how many would they have to cut before the ball hits the ground? Just one. The same is true with God's law. If you just broke only one part of it, you're guilty. You're a sinner. And you cannot be in His presence. Thankfully, that's not where it ends.

3. Sin leads to spiritual death, but Christ leads to spiritual life. The spiritual death will separate sinners from God to eternal hell, but Jesus paid the penalty so we can go to heaven.

"But God commendeth His love toward us, in that, while we were yet sinners, Christ died for us."
Romans 5:8

"For the wages of sin is death; but the gift of God is eternal life through Jesus Christ our Lord."
Romans 6:23

A price needed to be paid because of humanity's sin. It can be likened to someone committing a crime of property damage. Someone has to pay to repair the damage. But let's say it wasn't just any property that was damaged. Say it was something incredibly valuable, like the Eiffel Tower. If someone destroyed the Eiffel Tower, that would probably cost millions of dollars to replace. A price that most people cannot pay. When it comes to sin, the cost was even higher. Humanity in and of itself could not pay for the cost of redemption. We needed someone to pay the debt for us. That someone is Jesus Christ. He paid the price by being a sacrifice for humanity. He is God, which means He is perfect and able to pay the cost for sin. But He is also man, because only a man could redeem mankind. His innocent blood was shed in order to give everyone an opportunity to be forgiven of their debt.

4. Repent and place faith in Jesus. Believe that Jesus is the Son of God and claim the gift of eternal salvation that He offers you freely.

"For God so loved the world, that He gave His only begotten Son, that whosoever believeth in Him should not perish, but have everlasting life."
John 3:16

"Repent ye therefore, and be converted, that your sins may be blotted out, when the times of refreshing shall come from the presence of the Lord;" Acts 3:19.

"That if thou shalt confess with thy mouth the Lord Jesus, and shalt believe in thine heart that God hath raised Him from the dead, thou shalt be saved." Romans 10:9

This sounds too simple to a lot of people. But Jesus already did all of the work for us. All we need to do is accept the gift. Imagine that we are all on death row, but a pardon has been offered to everyone. All we need to do is accept the pardon, and we're set free. But we have the choice to also refuse the pardon. In history, there have been people placed on death row who were given a pardon from the president, yet they refused and were put to death anyway. The same is true for spiritual salvation. You can refuse it. But the consequence is eternal hell.

Again, I want to make it crystal clear that I'm not trying to force any of this upon you. I'm simply telling you this because I believe it to be true, and I don't want you to suffer a terrible fate of going to hell when you die. Now, I realize that this is not always what people want to hear, but you must understand my motives and that they are not malicious or deceptive in any sense. And I hope this hasn't come across as judgmental or unfeeling. I promise that is not my heart behind this. As a Christian, it is at the core of my belief that all people are bound for hell without Jesus Christ's gift of salvation. And I don't want you to suffer in hell for all eternity. I would like to see you in heaven someday.

Sincerely,
Nicholas M. Krohn.

About the Author

Nicholas M. Krohn has always had a love for both writing and the Lord. Nicholas received Jesus Christ as his Lord and Saviour at the age of nine, thanks to his faith-filled mother and a godly church. After his salvation, Nicholas spent most of his childhood free time jotting down fantastical stories that had a deep sense of Christianity within them. When he was a teenager, Nicholas discovered that writing was his calling from God.

While attending Heartland Baptist Bible College, Nicholas began seriously writing and self-publishing novels with the desire that they would both wholesomely entertain readers yet bring glory to God's name. It was here that he met his wife, Marissa, whom he married in 2017.

Halfway through college, Nicholas also realized that he could do more than just write Christian Fiction. After deep study in the Bible and graduating from Heartland Baptist Bible College in 2020, Nicholas made it his mission to not only point to the Lord with his fiction novels but to expound on the Word of God itself through commentaries, in-depth studies, and other such works of literature. Nicholas continues to pursue this work while living in Iowa with his wife and children.

Other Krohn'Stories Books

Marissa Krohn
The Silent Princess (children's book)

Nicholas M. Krohn

Baptist Apologetics
Baptist Apologetics: Volume One

Bible Commentary Series
Krohn's Commentary of the Book of Ruth
Krohn's Commentary of the First Book of Samuel
Krohn's Commentary of the Second Book of Samuel

The Scofield Series (Historical Fiction)
Scofield
Engel
Blume

The Zalian Chronicles (Christian Fantasy)
Heroes and Thieves I: The Noble Bandit
Heroes and Thieves II: A Bundle of Fools
Heroes and Thieves III: Clapia's Rebirth
Heroes and Thieves IV: Two Wastelands

Protector Editions
Heroes and Thieves: Protector Edition I

Krohn'Stories Poetry
Trains, Bridges, Cups, and Cheese
The Ramblings of a Cart Pusher

Standalone Novels
The Polish Ghost

Contact Us:

Website: krohnstories.storiad.com

Facebook Group: Krohn'Stories Books

Instagram: krohnstoriesbooks

Email: krohnstories@gmail.com

Fan mail inquiries, suggestions, and critiques are all welcome. We do our best to reply to all messages/emails but cannot promise due to a busy schedule. Please be appropriate. Any swearing, vulgarity, threatening, or otherwise inappropriate messages/emails will be deleted without any response.

www.ingramcontent.com/pod-product-compliance
Lightning Source LLC
Chambersburg PA
CBHW021426110726
47901CB00008B/2320